BURN

www.chellebliss.com
CHELLE BLISS
USA TODAY BESTSELLING AUTHOR

Publisher © Chelle Bliss December 10th 2019
Edited by Lisa A. Hollett
Proofread by iScream Proofread, Deaton Author Services, and Read By Rose
Cover Design © Chelle Bliss
Cover Model: Dylan Horsch
Cover Photo © Aaron Rogers & Dylan Horsch

Aunt Julie…
Thank you for just being you.
Sweet, loving, and supportive.

This one's for you.

Love, Chelle xoxo

Do you LOVE audiobooks?

LISTEN TO BURN NOW

Burn is now available in audiobook.
Visit *menofinked.com/burn* for more info.

Narrated by the amazingly talented
Jason Clarke and *Samantha Brentmoor*

1

GIGI

"What do you mean, that's your father?" I blink, my mouth hanging open as I gawk at Pike.

Holy freaking hell.

Pike glances up at me with those stormy green eyes, kneeling next to the guy who just tried to choke me to death. "Like, he's the guy who knocked up my mom."

"I know that, smartass," I snap. My body's wound so tight, the slightest touch would cause me to shatter into a million pieces.

He turns his gaze toward the asshole who attacked me. "What a fucking mess." Pike flicks his index finger against the guy's cheek, but he doesn't move. "But the bastard's out cold at least."

"Why was he in my apartment, choking me?" I

rub my neck, soothing the spot where his hands just were.

The reality of what happened starts to settle over me.

I was attacked.

Hell, if Pike hadn't have shown up when he did, I could have been… The thought is too much for me to even finish.

Pike rises to his feet and reaches for me, pulling my hand away from my neck. "I have no fucking idea why he was in your place, putting his hands on you." He cradles my face in his palms, and I move into his touch, needing the contact. "All I know is he'll never do it again."

I lock eyes with him, knowing he'd never let anyone hurt me. Especially a man whom he loathes.

My heart flutters and my knees wobble as the adrenaline from the fight starts to wear off. "Now what?" I ask, grabbing on to Pike's forearms, needing his support to stay upright.

Pike's eyes flash with concern as he slides his other arm behind my back, holding me. "Let's get you out of here."

I bat his hands away as he tries to lift me, and I finally find my legs again. "No. No." I motion toward the jagoff. "We can't just leave him here like this."

Pike draws in a slow breath. "He ain't going

anywhere, and I think it's best if you're not here when he wakes up."

I shake my head and point at the bastard. "I'm not leaving you here with *him*."

The corner of Pike's mouth turns up. "You worried about me, darlin'?"

I nod, unable to smile because there's a guy knocked out on my floor and what was supposed to be a kickass night has now turned into a clusterfuck. "If you're staying, I'm staying. You may need backup."

Pike bends his head back as he mutters a slew of curse words under his breath. I stand there, watching him talk to the ceiling.

How did I end up in this batshit crazy situation?

The answer is simple… Tequila.

"Should we get rid of him?" I let out a nervous laugh because I've watched way too many crime movies. "What am I saying? He's not dead."

Pike narrows his eyes as he dips his chin, studying me. "Who are you, and what have you done with Gigi?"

I punch his shoulder before sobering quickly. "This is no time for jokes. I don't know what we're supposed to do when something like this happens."

Pike strokes my cheek with his thumb. "And you think I know what to do in a situation like this?"

I lift a shoulder. "No, but the only people I know who would know what to do when bad shit like this goes down are my uncles. We could maybe…" I wince at the very thought of calling Uncle James or Uncle Thomas.

Pike closes his eyes, slowly shaking his head. "Fuck." His jaw tightens as he snarls. "The last thing I want is your family involved in my mess *again*."

Ugh. It's the last thing I want too, but I don't see another way out of this. We could call the FBI. They are looking for his dad, but after the way they treated Pike last time, I'm pretty sure that isn't an option he'd entertain.

I press my palm to his chest, looking into his big green eyes. "Then you better grab a shovel and be ready to dig a deep hole, because nothing happens in this town without my family knowing."

He shakes his head again like he can't believe the crazy shit coming out of my mouth. "Call James, then."

I'm out of his arms a second later, and I grab my phone off the floor. I can finally breathe for the first time since I stepped inside the apartment and the jackass lunged at me.

Thank God my dad and uncles taught me how to defend myself, or else… I shudder, trying to shake off what could've happened if I hadn't kept my head together and if Pike hadn't shown up when he did.

I dial the number which I've had on speed dial the

last week. I cringe on the first ring, knowing Uncle James is going to lose his shit.

"What's wrong?" he asks as soon as he answers.

No hello. No, hey kid, how ya doing? Nada. Nothing. Just, what's wrong?

Sweet baby Jesus.

"So, um…don't freak out," I warn.

"Just spill it, babe. I don't have all night."

"Umm. Pike's father is here," I blurt out, spilling the problem just like he asked. It's better to rip off the Band-Aid and get it over with, right?

"Is he secured?" is his only response.

I shrug like he can see me. *Secure?* I guess that's what you'd call him. He isn't going anywhere in a hurry. That much is true.

"Yeah. He's knocked out cold and taped up."

"Taped?" James pauses.

I meet Pike's eyes as he waits near the bedroom before answering, "Yeah. It's all we had, Uncle."

"Stay put, and for the love of God, don't call anyone else." There's a shuffling noise in the background followed by the sound of metal-on-metal. "Keep him there until we get there. We're nearby."

"Do you really have to bring Uncle Thomas?" I sigh, dropping my shoulders forward, knowing it's about to be a shitshow.

"Gigi," he says in a tone that tells me I'm not supposed to question him because he's the boss.

"Fine, Uncle James," I draw out, staring down the hallway again as Pike leans against the doorway of my bedroom. "We'll be here waiting. Need the address?"

"Already know it," he clips out.

Of course he does. He knows everything.

I don't even get a goodbye before the call ends. "He comin'?" Pike asks before I have a chance to lower the phone away from my face.

"They'll be here shortly. They're *nearby*." I use air quotes.

Pike lifts his arm, making a spot for me against his body as I walk back toward my bedroom. I slide underneath, tucking myself against him. "Do we just stand here?"

Pike gazes down at me, jaw tight, and the creases in his forehead deepen. "Maybe we should wait outside for them."

I curl my fingers into his T-shirt and rest my head on his chest. "James said to make sure he doesn't get away."

Pike dips his chin toward the motionless body. "Do you see the amount of tape I used on that asshole? He's not going anywhere, darlin'."

I grimace at the perfectly hog-tied man. "I wonder what they're going to do with him," I mumble.

"Don't give a fuck. They can throw his ass in the swamp for all I care."

I stiffen as the weight of his words slams into me. "Pike," I whisper, turning my gaze upward. "He's your dad. I'm sure you don't mean that."

"He was a sperm donor, Gigi. He's never been a dad. Never once has the man shown me any affection. Not once has he ever said a nice thing to me. He never gave a shit about me. So, why the hell should I care what happens to him?"

He has a point and every right to feel the way he does. Who am I to tell him otherwise? "Well..." I place my head on his chest again, thinking about his words. "I'm pretty sure they won't throw his ass in the swamp."

"Your uncles are pretty badass."

I lean my head back, smiling up at him. Pike's a lot like them. All rough edges with a soft center.

"We're going to have to do something about this apartment," Pike says, trying to distract me from the reality that's lying near our feet.

"What do you mean?" I glance around, taking in the white walls, tile floor, and not much else. The place is empty. A completely blank canvas waiting for me to get my ass in gear and decorate.

"You need furniture," he states the obvious.

"I know. I just got the keys before we were hauled off to the Disciples' compound, and now this." I wave my hand toward his father. "Someday, things will calm down enough for me to make this place a home."

He curls his hand around my shoulder and holds me tighter to his chest, stroking my exposed flesh with his thumb. "I'll help you."

We're standing in what's going to be my bedroom, his dad lying motionless and bound, talking about moving like it's just another day and nothing out of the ordinary has happened.

The man could've killed me.

I could be the one lying on the floor, not moving, not breathing. If Pike had waited just a few more minutes, I probably would be.

Jesus.

My skin crawls at the reality. I was so busy going through the motions after Pike stormed in, beating the hell out of the guy, I hadn't really let that sink in.

Pike's fingers continue to stroke my skin as I start to have another internal freak-out. "Next day off, we'll get a truck and grab whatever you need at the store."

"I can do it myself. It's not that big a deal." Nothing seems like a big deal anymore after what just happened. What's a little furniture compared to dying?

Pike takes a step back, staring down at me as he rests his hands on my shoulders. The look on his face is serious and fierce. "Babe," he snaps.

"Yeah?" I find the edge of his shirt with my

fingers, shoving them under the soft material as I tilt my head back, looking up at him. "What?"

"*We're* doing it," he tells me like he's the boss.

I narrow my eyes. "I didn't see your name on the lease, and last time I checked, I can do things on my own."

His eyes match my own as we eyeball each other in a virtual pissing match. "Have you always been this hardheaded?"

I nod, smiling. "Pretty much," I mutter.

Pike wraps his arms around me, turning our bodies so he's facing his father and I'm not. "You're fuckin' crazy," he tells me like I don't already know this.

I bury my face in his chest, wishing I'd just gone to his place like he'd asked. We wouldn't be standing here, waiting for my uncles, with his father hog-tied on the floor.

But then again, would his father have been here when I did eventually come back to the apartment?

I tighten my fingers around the material of his shirt, staring blankly at the wall as I shiver. "It's a good thing you love crazy, then."

There's a pounding on the front door, making us jump. "Open up, kid!"

"Seriously, did they fly here?" Pike asks.

"They said they were close, and I guess they weren't lying." I pull out of his embrace, squaring my shoulders like I'm preparing for battle. "Here we go. You ready?" I ask and get a quick nod from Pike.

When I open the door, Uncle James and Uncle Thomas are standing next to each other, lips pinched, foreheads crinkled, looking badass and pissed off like they always do. It's their thing, and they've perfected it.

"Where is he?" Uncle Thomas asks, pushing past me without as much as a hello.

These men.

"In the back." I pitch my thumb over my shoulder, but only Uncle James is still in front of me.

James's eyes sweep across my body as he steps inside. "You okay?"

I nod, not saying anything because I don't know exactly how I feel. I'm physically okay, but being attacked has a way of changing a person on the inside.

I feel different.

I'm numb. That's the only way I can describe how I've felt for the last handful of minutes. Maybe I'm in shock. It's not every day I see my life flash before my eyes. "Yeah," I answer slowly and softly, but not believing my own words, which means he doesn't buy them either.

James squints and reaches out, running his finger along my neck where Pike's Dad's hands had been. "We'll talk about this later."

"Later?" I gulp, but I shouldn't be worried. I'm the victim here, and even if I weren't, Uncle James would always protect me.

"Later. Got shit to do." He drops his hand and stalks right by me, heading toward the back of the apartment as I follow him.

When we enter the room, Thomas is crouched down, rolling the big jerk to his side. "You did good with the tape, kid."

Pike rubs his neck, giving Thomas a halfhearted smile. "I wish I could say it was the first time I'd ever tied someone up," Pike confesses before his eyes dart to me.

I rock back on my heels at that little revelation. Pike's tied someone up before? I'd be fooling myself if I thought his life was easy breezy. After all, he did end up with the Disciples after getting shot. I knew it wasn't all sunshine and rainbows, but there are so many bits and pieces of his life I am missing.

I mean, at no time in my life have I ever had to tie someone up. Never. Not even one of my little sisters when they were being a total pain in my ass…which, let me tell you, was often.

I should've known it wasn't his first time because he didn't even pause for a moment as he wound the tape around his father's arms and legs, securing him easily. But I was so inside my own head about what had just happened, I didn't give it a single thought.

James steps closer, getting his first look at the man's face. "Damn, you got a few good shots in too. Nice touch."

"I wasn't going to let him hurt her again." Pike reaches out, wraps his hand around my arm, and pulls me toward him.

I tuck myself against his body, groaning into his T-shirt. "I'm fine."

James grunts before he pulls a knife from his back pocket and cuts the tape away from the guy's hands and feet. "I'll carry the top. You get the bottom, Thomas."

"I'm too old for this shit," Thomas mutters under his breath before he bends over and grabs Colton's feet.

"I can do it," Pike offers, stepping forward as he moves me out of his embrace.

Thomas lifts his head, his eyes blazing with anger. "Are you saying we're too frail to carry a man?"

Oh dear God. My eyes widen as I rock backward on my heels, sucking in a breath.

"No, sir," Pike replies quickly, realizing his error, and he steps back toward me. "I figured it's my mess and I should help clean it up."

"Don't listen to him." James climbs to his feet, waving off Thomas before leveling Pike with his steely gaze. "This is not *your* mess. This is *our* mess. You stay here and look after Gigi. Take her to your place for the night. This isn't the first guy we've carried, and I'm sure it won't be the last. We'll deal with your father alone."

Not the first guy we've carried. My mouth falls open. Those words make me look at my badass uncles in a whole new light. I always knew they'd done things, but I never put much thought into what exactly that meant…until now.

"What are you going to do with him?" I ask, watching my uncles as they glance at each other.

"We're not going to make him disappear or anything." Thomas laughs like the very thought is absurd, and for a moment, I'm relieved.

"Yeah, that would be *illegal*," James adds, dropping his voice in a weird way, causing me to blink.

My mind may not be working right, but I don't miss the awkwardness. Are my uncles really the type of men who could make a person disappear?

"What?" I blurt out because they are truly scary right now. I don't know how I've never seen this side of them before, but now it's slapping me right in the face.

Holy shit.

"Everyone's living, sweetheart," Thomas says gently, trying to calm my fears. "We're going to haul his ass down to the FBI headquarters and drop him. They can sort his shit out."

Maybe I overreacted, jumping to conclusions and

taking their words a little too literally. I never really thought they had bad in them, but then again…they were well acquainted with men like Tiny.

"I know. I didn't really think you were going to throw his ass in the swamp for the alligators to eat." I snort, knowing I sounded like an idiot.

"We'd never do such a thing." James gives Thomas the side-eye as he reaches down to grab the guy's arms. "Thomas, legs, man. Let's get this shit done and over so I can get home before the sun comes up."

Thomas groans as he grabs ahold of the asshole's ankles. "I fucking hate the FBI. They're going to have a million questions. Can't we just drop him at the sheriff's office and be done?"

James grunts. "I already told the Feds I don't have time for their shit. They just want him and said they could give two fucks what we had to say."

I gaze up at Pike as they carry his father toward the hallway. "Do you want to go with them?"

Pike wraps his arm around me, moving our bodies to follow them. "No way, darlin'. I'm not leaving your side tonight."

"I'm okay," I whisper even though I feel the weight of the last half hour starting to press down on me like a wet blanket.

Pike stops, places his fingers under my chin, and brings my eyes to his. "I'm not leaving you. I don't want to say it again. I'm right where I want to be." He ticks his chin toward my uncles. "Plus, they officially scare the shit out of me. They're good men, Gigi. You're lucky they have your back."

"I know," I whisper and want to remind him they have his too, but I don't have a chance before Thomas's groan has us turning our heads.

"I forgot how dead weight is so fucking hard to carry," James groans.

Pike and I watch in sheer fascination as they carry him through the doorway, almost knocking his head against the frame.

"Are you done moaning, or do you want to draw the neighbors' attention while we carry him out of our niece's apartment?" Thomas lurches to a stop, Colton's feet in his hands.

James glares at Thomas, muttering something under his breath. "I'm done, old fucker. Get moving."

Thomas grunts, trying to get a better hold on the guy's ankles and almost dropping him as they clear the doorway. "You're chattering on like a lonely old woman."

"Are they always like this?" Pike asks as we follow them outside, keeping our distance.

"Sometimes, they're worse," I tell him, tucking my thumb into the waistband of his pants as we walk.

"We don't need you two watching over us. Take her to your place, Pike." James moves his head toward

Pike's apartment. "Get settled and get some rest. We'll talk tomorrow."

"Fucking great," Pike mutters, glancing down at me. "That should be fun."

"They're all bark and no bite, baby." I smile up at him, hoping my words are true. "They're gentle giants."

"Who have carried bodies before," he reminds me as if I could actually forget their earlier words, which I haven't.

I place my hand on Pike's chest. "Don't worry about them. You're one of us now."

Pike's eyes flash, but whatever my words stir in him is instantly hidden. Like it or not, Pike is now in the fold. My family is just as wrapped up as he is in whatever his father brought to our doorstep.

"Let's get you to bed," he says, skipping over my statement.

I sigh but nod, because nothing sounds better. "This evening was supposed to end like that, but way sexier."

"There's always tomorrow, darlin'." He stops near his doorway, his gaze trained on James and Thomas as they carry the asshole toward the car. "And I'm not sure about being one of you, especially after your father hears about tonight."

I stare at my uncles as my stomach tightens. "You let me handle my father."

"I need to be a man and deal with him myself, Gigi. It's the only way I have any hope of earning his respect."

"Fine," I whisper. My dad's liable to pop a freaking vein when he hears about tonight, but so be it. "But just so you know, it's going to suck."

"I never thought it would be easy."

2

PIKE

"SAY THAT AGAIN." Gigi's father turns his head, giving me his ear like he didn't hear every word I'd just spoken.

I cross my arms, standing on the other side of his desk, and look him straight in the eyes. "My father was in Gigi's apartment last night," I repeat, giving him what he wants.

Joe pinches the bridge of his nose and grimaces like he's just eaten a steamy pile of horseshit. "And…" His jaw ticks.

This isn't going to go down the way I'd hoped. I don't know what I was thinking. I knew it wasn't going to be easy, but fuck, I'm not sure I've ever had a tougher conversation.

I remind myself I'm talking to Gigi's father and

not my boss. He's worried about his little girl, which is understandable and expected.

"He attacked Gigi, but she was able to fight him off. I knocked him out before he could do anything worse." I swallow hard, trying not to think about what could've happened if I hadn't…

He closes his eyes and grits his teeth. "And…"

Jesus Christ.

Almost-silent Joe is far scarier than ranting-and-raving Joe. I know how to handle men with bad tempers and loud mouths, but the silent types…those are wild cards.

"And we called Thomas and James afterward. They took him to the FBI, where he is now, and where he will stay for the foreseeable future."

Joe stares up at me, his blue eyes burning with nothing short of rage. He closes his hand into a tight fist against the armrest of his chair and flexes. "So, my kid was attacked because…" His voice trails off.

I'm sure he's fighting the urge to beat my face to a bloody pulp. He wants me to say it's my fault. He wants me to tell him I brought this trouble to her doorstep.

And, in all honesty, I did.

"Because my father's an asshole," I blurt out, giving him what I can but not what he wants. "I don't know why he was at her place, but he was, and I handled it."

"Giovanna!" Joe yells so loudly, my ears ring. "Get your ass in here."

"I don't think…" My words die in my mouth from the murderous look he throws my way.

He stands quickly, leaning over his desk with his knuckles against the wood, coming eye-to-eye with me. "That's the problem, Pike. You don't think. My kid could've been killed last night because of you. No. Scratch that." He shakes his head, grinding his teeth together until they squeak. "She could've been killed twice since you walked into her life."

I jerk back my head like he punched me in the face. His words sting, but they're true.

"Daddy," Gigi hisses like he's gone off the rails. "What the hell is wrong with you?"

He turns his head toward the doorway but doesn't back away from my space. "What's wrong with me?"

She nods.

He lifts a hand and touches his chest. "What's wrong with me?" he repeats in a deeper and scarier than shit tone.

She pushes her long brown hair behind her shoulder before crossing her arms, giving him the same look he's giving her. "Yeah, Dad. You're in here freaking out so loud the entire shop—which is full of customers, by the way—can hear you. You're like a raving lunatic."

Joe stiffens and gawks at Gigi. "I'm a lunatic?"

She nods again, pinching her lips as her glare holds steady. "You're acting like one."

I scrub my hand down my face, muttering to myself. "Fuck me."

Joe takes a step back, hands balled at his sides, chest heaving like he's about to blow a gasket. "I'm sorry I'm losing my shit, but you were almost killed twice because of—" he turns his gaze toward me and snarls "—him."

"Give us a few minutes, darlin'," I tell her when she's about to open her mouth and probably say something she'll regret later.

Her icy gaze sweeps over me, searching my face like she's not sure it's a good idea. This conversation needs to be handled man-to-man. Joe and I need to have a straight and to the point conversation about what went down and my feelings for his daughter.

Gigi shakes her head as her eyes go back to her dad. "I can't deal with this." She throws her arm out, waving her hand at us. "You two work it out. I don't want to hear any more yelling, and, Dad…" She waits, cocking her head at him until he finally looks at her. "Don't walk out of this room until you've calmed down and have started acting like a rational human being again."

We gawk at her as she stalks out of the room, high heels clicking down the hallway toward the shop, showing just how badass she is.

"Fuck, I liked her so much better when she was five," he groans and collapses back in the chair.

I try to imagine Gigi as a little thing all full of sass and sweetness. God, she had to have this man wrapped around her little finger from the moment she was born.

"Someday, when you have children of your own, you'll understand how I'm feeling, Pike. From the moment you walked into her life, you've brought nothing but danger and misery." He shakes his head slowly, eyes narrowed on me like a hawk. "I can't give my blessing for whatever you two have going on. I just can't do it."

I suck in a deep breath, figuring there's no better time than now to lay it all out for him. "We've seen a lot of shit in the last week. We've lived even more, Joe." I take the seat across from him, leaning back, trying to be chill as fuck. "I can't stop bad things from happening, but I can promise to keep her safe. I'd do anything in my power to protect her. Hell, I'd take a bullet for her without even blinking."

"You know most men don't have to worry about taking a bullet for their girl? Normal people don't worry about being gunned down." He raises an eyebrow.

He's right, but I can't change the cards I've been dealt. I can't change the past I was born into. All I can do is try to control the damage from the insane shit-show I tried to leave behind me.

"Would you rather see Gigi with some stiff suit who goes to an office all day, working long hours, probably fucking his secretary because he's a sleazy asshole? You'd want her with someone who doesn't have a loyal bone in his body?"

Joe studies me, not speaking for what seems like forever. "Of course I don't want that for my daughter, but I also want someone who doesn't have his past chasing him into his future."

I run my fingers through my hair, keeping my voice calm and low. "It's my father's past. Not mine," I correct him. "You're judging me for things outside of my control. Things that happened when I was a kid. A goddamn kid, Joe!"

He flinches as I bark out the last statement, but that doesn't stop me. I have to hold my ground now or risk being run over for the rest of my life.

"I don't know what it's like to grow up Gallo, surrounded by people who love you. People who are only looking out for your well-being all the goddamn time. People who will always have your back." I run my sweaty palms down the front of my jeans and take a deep breath. "I never had anyone besides my gran who gave two shits about me. Do you know what it's like to be that alone? Not knowing love or safety, even as a child?"

I pause for only a second, and when he starts to open his mouth, I continue.

"I do. I never had anyone but myself to fall back on. I never had Sunday dinners, big family Christmases, birthday parties, or things most people get to experience in life. I had shit and I came from shit, but now, I'm trying to break free. Start over. Become someone better than my past. Someone different."

I hold up my hand because I want him to hear it all, and the last thing I want is him interrupting me.

"The fact that you'd hold their sins against me, telling me to stay away from your daughter because of things outside my control, is pure and utter bullshit. I thought you were a better man. I thought you were a fair man. I thought you were…"

"Stop," he growls.

"I'm not finished." I raise my chin defiantly.

"You spoke. Now, it's my turn," he argues, rubbing his face. "Kids never stop giving stress and heartache. I don't care how old she is, I'll always worry about her." He twists his hands together, eyes trained on me. "Am I just supposed to turn that off?"

I lift a shoulder and shake my head. "She never should have been wrapped up in my father's business. All I can say is I'm sorry." I glance down as I grip my knee, trying to stop it from shaking. "No matter how much I try to leave them behind, all their hate and bullshit—somehow, it follows me." I gaze at him again. “You worry about Gigi constantly. There’s never been a day when my parents have worried about me. Never been a day when they gave two shits if I was alive and breathing. Never been a moment when they wondered how something would affect me and my brother. They are vile, worthless, and selfish people, but no matter how hard I try to break free, their bullshit follows.”

Joe passes his hand over his lips, his fingers rubbing the stubble along his jaw. “You had a bad life.”

“I have a great life now, but I had a shit childhood,” I correct him.

“No one should have the sins of their father follow them. No one should have to worry about whether or not they’ll be able to take their next breath because of a deal their father made.”

I hold Joe’s gaze. “With him in FBI custody, DiSantis dead, and my mother not breathing, I’m hoping it’s all behind me.”

A shadow passes across Joe’s features as he shakes his head. “I’m sorry about your mom.”

I want to say I’m not sorry because, well, I’m not. It’s cold, callous, and a shitty thing to think, but the woman never gave a damn about me. Why should I give a single shit about her?

“Will you be heading up to Tennessee to handle her affairs?” he asks when I don’t reply.

I blink a few times, eyebrows drawn down, wondering if that's what I'm supposed to do? Is that what a person does in my situation?

"Possibly," I tell him because I have no idea what someone does after a family member dies.

"Take as much time as you need," he offers with so much kindness in his voice, I'm completely thrown off.

Then it clicks.

He's trying to get rid of me.

"I have to talk to my gran, but I'm sure I'll only be gone a couple of days. My brother and Gran should be able to handle everything without me. They've been getting by without me for years."

Joe leans forward, resting his elbows on the desk. "Does he live with your grandmother?"

I nod. "He does since my mother…"

"Gotcha. Well, let me clue you in on a few things. As a man with a few brothers, I can tell you your brother is not okay. Your brother needs you more than anyone else has ever needed you."

He does? I haven't given much thought to Austin since hearing about my mother. "You think?"

"Death has a way of changing someone. Especially when it's the death of someone you love. You may not have any good feelings for your parents, but maybe Austin does. He's trying to work through those feelings, and it's not easy for him at his age. Hell, it's not easy at any age. He'll need your strength to help him through this time."

"We haven't been tight in years." Ten years, to be exact. I hadn't seen Austin since I'd blown town, leaving my parents and everything else in my life behind.

"You're blood. Tight or not, he's going to need you. This is going to give him a reality check. Don't you remember when you were his age and you thought you were untouchable? This is going to have him facing his mortality."

I lean back, exhaling and coming to terms with shit I hadn't thought about. "Yeah," I whisper.

Their darkness clung to me, became part of me. I'd spent ten years trying to break free from that time in my life. From the hate they gave freely and only showed to me.

Why? I have no fucking clue. But at this point in my life, I don't give a fuck anymore.

But at Austin's age, I was angry. I wanted the world to feel the pain I felt.

"You're going to need more than a few days to sort him out. Don't rush back on our account. We'll handle your appointments. Izzy will reschedule your clients, so you don't have to worry about anything except spending time with your family."

"Thanks." I dip my head, trying to be gracious but knowing he's not going to all this trouble out of the goodness of his heart. "Now, can we talk about the giant elephant in the room?"

Joe lifts his chin, twisting his lips as he pulls at the collar of his black T-shirt. "I'm not happy about it."

"About us being together?"

"About everything," he answers in a flat tone. "About what happened in Daytona. About the bullets and your father. About everything," he repeats.

I lean forward, resting my elbows on my knees, and look him right in the eyes. "I can't change what happened, but I can make sure nothing like that ever touches her again. I can love her like no one else ever can or will. I can make her happier than anyone else has before. Hell—" I pause for a moment and lean back. "I already have."

He draws in a deep breath before sighing. "When I thought about my little girl growing up, I never pictured her with a guy like you. I thought she'd find a college boy, settle down, and have a family. I never pictured her running for her life, hiding in a goddamn closet as bullets were flying."

I can see he's not going to get over that little event. It's burned into his brain, and when he looks at me, all he sees is someone who brought that to his daughter's door.

"Shit happens." I don't have the flashy cars and big bank account, but fuck, I do the best I can with what I have. "I may not have grown up surrounded by expensive things and the love of my parents, but I'm a good man, Joe."

He grunts as I sit up straighter, winding myself up for the big finish.

"I work hard. I do the right thing. I protect those I love, even if it costs me my life. I would've gladly jumped in front of a bullet for your daughter. I'd do anything to keep her safe and happy. I'm sorry if that's not good enough for you, but the only person who will decide if Gigi's going to be my girl is Gigi. No one else." I touch my chest. "Not me." Then I point at him. "Not you. Not your wife. Not anyone else in this shop. Only Gigi." I pitch my thumb toward the door, driving the point home.

Joe snaps his head back like I've slapped him. "You're suddenly very wordy, kid." The corners of his mouth curve up ever so slightly, and for a minute, I feel like I'm getting somewhere.

There're two ways this conversation can go… He'll back off and give us space, or he'll come down harder, trying to push a wedge between us just to show how much pull he has over his daughter.

I'm not trying to fuck with their relationship to save ours. That's the last thing I want to do. Gigi has something special with her father—hell, with her whole family—and I'd never let her throw all that away for someone like me.

"I can't punch your ass out, so I gotta fight you

with the only thing I have." I shrug, giving him a smug grin. "You can say whatever you'd like to me about our relationship, about me, about your displeasure at the entire situation. I'm grown. I can handle it. But just to clue you the fuck in, she's grown too."

Joe's eyes widen, but I don't let his shock stop me. "I respect you, man. I respected you before I ever stepped foot in Inked. I respect you even more after watching you with your family. The depth to which you love them is something I strive to find and hold on to in my life. The last thing I want is you as an enemy."

He opens his mouth again, but I shake my head. "I tried to end things with your daughter after we left the Disciples' compound. She wasn't having any of it. You know how she is. She's going to dig her heels in and do whatever the hell she wants, no matter what either one of us says or thinks."

I tilt my head, waiting for his response. He seems surprised by my words, almost taken aback by them as he watches me without moving a muscle.

I can take his anger.

I can deal with his disdain for our relationship.

The one thing I know I can't take is his silence. "I..."

"Shut up," he rasps.

I snap my mouth shut as I lean over my legs. The

man has finally found his words, and I am not about to stop him from talking.

"Suzy lost it on me this morning." He digs his fingers into his forehead and frowns. "She told me to get my head out of my ass and let Giovanna live her own life. Don't get me wrong. Suzy's not happy about what went down in the last week. She's petrified. But she said the same thing you just did, only without all the veiled threats and profanity."

"We good in here?" a female voice asks.

We turn our heads to the doorway, finding Izzy watching us. "We're good," he answers, waving her away with his hand.

"You sure?" Her eyes are on me now like she's not buying the line Joe's selling.

"Yeah," I tell her. "We're almost done."

"You both have clients out here waiting while you two girls talk about love and relationships. Wrap it up, boys," she warns before she stalks down the hallway, heels clicking against the tile just like Gigi's did.

Joe swivels his chair from side to side and sighs. "I don't like the entire situation. All I want is for my daughter to be happy."

"She is."

"For her to have someone she can count on. For her to have someone who will love her more than himself. I'm not yet convinced that man is you, Pike."

"It is," I argue. *Fuck me.* I just about jumped in

front of a goddamn bullet for her. How much more does the man want?

"All I know is that you *met* my kid in Daytona, and now you're here. But you're right…"

Finally.

"I can't control her. I can't tell her what to do anymore. She's grown. She has a mind of her own and has since she was a little girl. I don't have to like what's going on between the two of you. I never will. But I know the harder I pull her away, the tighter she'll cling to you."

He runs his hand back through his hair, grinding his teeth, and I stay silent. I've said all I needed to, and now it's up to him to say what he needs to in order to be at peace with the situation.

"Go back to Tennessee and let things calm down around here. Let me get over the panic of almost losing my daughter. Give me time to sort my shit out, and we'll see how I feel then. I've always tried to be fair. I know not everyone grows up blessed with good parents and a big family. I know you've been given a shit hand to start out, but now's your time to make your own path and change the course your life has been on."

"It's what I've been trying to do for ten years now, Joe. Coming here, to Inked, is my chance to start over and find my place in this world. I want to leave all the baggage of my past in the past. I want what I've never had."

He stands, cracking his knuckles. "I may not approve of you with my daughter, but that doesn't mean I don't respect you for what you're trying to do with your life."

"Enough!" Gigi hollers, stalking into the room and coming to stand by the side of the desk near her father. "And, Daddy—" she turns her gaze toward him, straightening her back "—just so you know, I'm going to Tennessee with Pike."

He opens his mouth, but she shakes her head, narrowing her eyes.

"I don't want to hear it." Gigi reaches for my hand, and I give it to her, squeezing it tightly. "Izzy's going to reschedule my clients. I could use a few days away from the craziness to get my head on straight. Pike needs someone with him when he buries his mother, and I'm going to be that person. Got it?"

Joe blinks a few times, stunned. "Yes, baby girl."

"Good." She smiles, turning her attention back toward me. "Let's finish up today, and then we'll go. I'm sure your gran and brother need you up there as soon as possible."

"I suppose so," I mumble, rubbing the back of my neck, blown away by the backbone on my girl.

"Then it's settled. We'll leave in the morning," she tells me.

"Maybe Pike wants to visit his family alone," Joe inserts, still trying to put that space between us.

Gigi drops a shoulder, cocking her head to the side, gaze sweeping across his face. "Would you want Ma with you if something happened to Grandma or Grandpa?"

Joe nods, frowning. "I couldn't imagine handling anything without her."

"Point proven." She raises her palm like she knows he's about to say something else. "I don't want to hear how it's different, Daddy. It's not. No one should have to go through something like this alone."

"All right," he mumbles, shocking the shit out of me—and her too, by the way her head jerks back ever so slightly. "You go up there with him."

"Thank you." She pulls me toward the door, leaving her father still standing by his desk. When we're in the hall, she turns back to face him. "And, Daddy…" She pauses.

"Yeah?"

"I wasn't asking your permission."

My eyes widen, and I bite my lip to stop myself from laughing. This chick is all sass and attitude.

She's not scared of anyone.

Not even her father.

3

GIGI

"Do you want to have two visitations or only one?" Pike's granny asks over the phone.

I keep my eyes on my truck, trying not to be too nosy, but it's not easy as we walk through the parking lot of the fast-food restaurant. I sip my soda, pretending not to listen to their conversation but hearing every word.

He'd spoken to her before we left Florida and there didn't seem to be any tension between them, but now, with the talk of his mother's funeral, the uneasiness in their voices is hard to miss.

"No. I don't even know why we're having one. Why the hell would we do two?" Pike glances at me as he runs his hand through his light-brown hair, letting out a low grunt.

I give him a tight smile, straw between my teeth, somehow stopping myself from telling him to chill out. This is about his mother after all, but the hatred runs deep. Even after her death, the way Pike feels about her hasn't changed at all.

"Don't start with me, child. There are people in this community who would like to pay their respects. Now, pick. One or two?"

"One," he growls.

"How hard was that?" Her voice is full of sarcasm.

Pike scowls. "Can't we discuss this when we get there?"

"The funeral home needs to finalize their calendar. You never know who's going to die today and steal our place if we don't get on their schedule now."

Pike fishes the keys from his pocket and presses the button, unlocking the doors. "Don't give a damn when we do it. Don't give a shit how many time slots we have. I just want to get it over with." He leans against the back of the truck, resting his arms over the bed, staring off into the distance.

I stand next to him, sucking down the last drops of my soda, eyes on him. The closer we get to his hometown, the crankier he becomes. This short conversation with his granny has him on edge, and I'm pretty sure it's only going to get worse. Pike has a cold streak, and right now, he's the freaking Arctic.

"This isn't about you, Pike. What about Austin?"

Snap. Gran has a point.

Pike closes his eyes and sucks in a breath at the mention of his little brother. "I get it. I do. If it's important to him, ask him and not me."

I grimace, turning my face so he can't see. Man, he needs to calm down, take a step back, and look at it from his brother's perspective.

"We have enough sad things going on over here. You better get your head on straight before you walk into this house. Leave your past at the door and think about your brother. He's a kid, and he's just lost the one person who loved him the most. You got me?"

The lines across Pike's forehead deepen. "Loud and clear. We'll be there in a few hours and can discuss everything then."

"I can't wait to see you. But do me a favor…" She pauses for only a second. "Leave your attitude in Georgia."

I let out a little laugh, covering my mouth with my hand as he glances at me.

"Fuck," he hisses, lifting his face toward the sky and closing his eyes. "What a damn mess."

I slide my hand across his back and step closer. I'm not sure what to do in a situation like this, but I want to be there for him. "Everything's going to be okay," I tell him, trying to comfort whatever demons are chasing him.

He leans his head down toward me, eyes blazing with so many emotions. "It's all so fucked up."

Beyond fucked up. "I know."

Nothing's been normal since the moment Pike walked back into my life. I've experienced more crazy things in the last week than I had in my entire twenty-something years being alive. He's definitely not wrong when he says things are so *fucked up*. Everything has been.

Pike wraps his arms around my waist, pulling me tight against his body. "I'm sorry I brought you along. You don't need to be witness to all this."

I stick my hand under his T-shirt, running my fingernails across the skin of his lower back and smashing my cheek against his hard chest. "I want to be here," I murmur into his T-shirt.

His lips are against my hair. "You deserve happiness and the fairy-tale family you have, Gigi. Mine is awful. The Moores are nothing like the Gallos. I never meant to pull you into the drama and bullshit."

"We aren't perfect either, Pike," I remind him. "No family is. Sure, we seem like a freaking Norman Rockwell painting on the outside, but we fight all the time and crazy shit happens in our lives too."

"Darlin', your family almost shits rainbows."

Oh no, he didn't. I tip my head back, nose scrunched up, and glare at him. "Do you really believe that?"

Pike nods, his strong hands splayed out across my

back. "Never met a family quite like yours. They love each other. They'll do anything for each other. They argue sometimes, sure, but there's lots of love there."

I step back, gawking at him. I shouldn't be surprised that with the parents he had, the man has no perception of an average family. "That's how family works."

"That's how *your* family works."

I cock my head and cross my arms. "And you know the inner workings of families because…"

I shouldn't have said it. It was wrong of me to throw his fucked-up childhood in his face, but I couldn't stop myself. I can only hold my tongue so long before I snap. Talking about my family is the quickest way to get me to start spewing words before thinking.

He shrugs. "I don't know. The short time I've been with the Gallos, I just…"

"Choose your words very carefully," I warn him, ready to give him an even bigger piece of my mind.

I can put up with his shitty attitude.

I can even put up with his anger.

The one thing I can't put up with is him throwing digs at my family.

He takes a deep breath and lets out a sigh. "You look at my family and think, wow, they're so messed up, right?"

"Not really," I lie.

I'm not sure "messed up" is even a strong enough term to describe the Moores. I'll never know his mother, but in the small amount of time I spent with his father…he tried to freaking kill me. His granny and Austin are complete unknowns, but they won't be for too much longer.

Pike eyes me like he knows I'm not being truthful. "You're a shit liar." He shakes his head with a small smirk on his lips. "Maybe the worst ever."

I laugh with a shrug. "I didn't want to hurt your feelings."

"Let's go." He motions toward the cab of the truck. "I want to get there before nightfall."

I take a step backward, but his hand captures mine before I get too far. I squeak as my body jolts, and he pulls me against him again. "Promise you won't hate me after this trip," he begs, his eyes searching mine.

"I won't." I blink a few times, confused. "Why would I?"

He places his palms against my face as he traces the edge of my jaw with his thumbs. "When you see where I come from and the few family members I have left, you may not like what you come across. Sometimes it's easier to cut dead weight than wade through the mess, even if there could be something great on the other side."

"Are you the something great?" I tease him.

"We're the something great." He doesn't even crack a smile when he says the words.

I can't stop my stupid smile from spreading. I place my hand on his chest right over his heart. "We've already been through some ugly things together, Pike, but I'm still here."

He rests his forehead against mine, hands still cupping my cheeks. "Thank fuck for small miracles," he mutters.

I don't speak, letting him feel whatever he's feeling. I just breathe him in, seeing the sadness marring his features.

He opens his eyes, locking on mine. "I take back what I said earlier."

"What?" I whisper, gripping his T-shirt in my hands.

"I'm glad you're coming with me. I'm not sure I could face this alone," he confesses.

And just like that, arctic Pike is gone and the guy I love is back.

"There's nowhere else I'd rather be. I'd never let you go through this alone," I reply.

Not that long ago, I wanted nothing more than to send him back to Daytona. I couldn't believe he showed up at Inked out of the clear blue and that it wasn't intentional. But after everything we've been through, his arrest, our stay at the compound, and then almost getting killed, I feel territorial about him.

I have an insatiable need to make sure he's okay and to be at his side, which I've never experienced.

Pike's fingers are on my chin, lifting my mouth to his. The kiss is whisper-soft but filled with all the sweetness of the moment. I could stay like this forever, peppering him with gentle kisses.

Life is simple in that moment.

There's nothing trying to pull us apart. No one chirping in our ears about how we're wrong for each other or trying to end our lives.

"We better go." He pulls his head back, ending the kiss. "Granny's waiting, and if she's bitchy now, the longer she waits, the bitchier she'll become."

Just great. "She sounds like Maria."

"Constance may be worse," he says, finally dropping his hand and breaking our connection.

I back away, moving slowly and keeping my eyes on him as I make my way around the side of the truck. "Then why are we still here? It's bad enough I'm meeting your grandmother under these circumstances, I don't want to make her wait any longer. I need her to like me, Pike."

"Why?" he asks as he slides into the truck, and I climb in next to him. "All that matters is I like you."

I turn, blinking at him like he understands nothing

about me even after everything we've been through. "Are you new?"

He furrows his eyebrows as he turns the key in the ignition, facing me. "Am I new?"

I nod quickly. "Uh, you know family's important. Like, *the* most important thing to me. Not just my family, but yours too. If your grandmother hates me…" I pause and shake my head because the look he's giving me says he doesn't really understand me at all. "Let's go." I motion toward the windshield. "I'll explain as you drive. We're wasting daylight."

"We're only three hours away," he tells me like that's supposed to make all the difference in the world.

I cross my arms over my chest, pinching my lips together, and eyeball him.

"Okay. Okay." He slings his arm across the back of my seat, pulling out of the parking spot faster than I expect.

Sheesh. Pike Moore doesn't like being told what to do.

I lean against the door, turning my face toward him, wishing I could smack the shit out of him.

"What?" He gives me the side-eye.

I slowly shake my head, telling myself he's going through a lot of shit, and take a deep breath before I say something I know I'll regret. I should give him a break. Let him throw whatever fit he's throwing to get the emotion out. I know there's a lot he's feeling and not sharing.

"Back to the family part," I explain in a calm, even tone. "It's important to me that your grandmother, and even Austin, likes me. Just like it's important to me that my family likes you."

"I think we burned that bridge." He doesn't even look at me when he says that.

"Which one?" I narrow my eyes, feeling my heart starting to race.

His eyes cut to mine as we sit at the red light, waiting to pull onto the highway. "Your family, especially your father, will never like me."

"That's not true," I argue.

He's facing forward again, checking the side mirror before the light turns green. "The conversation I had with your father yesterday was anything but friendly."

"He'll get over the shock of what happened and move on."

Pike lets out a bitter laugh. "I've known a lot of men like your father, and one thing they don't do is get over shit and move on, especially when it involves their wife or kids."

I stare out the windshield, trying to relax my jaw but failing. "My father isn't like most men," I grumble.

"You got that shit right," Pike says quickly. "He's worse."

I snap my eyes to him, dropping my hands to my lap and clenching them into tight fists. "I've known that man my entire life. He *will* get over this, and as soon as he knows you like I do, he'll even like you too. But if you keep acting like a shithead…"

"You're fooling yourself, darlin'." His eyes flicker to mine. "Your dad and I will never be friends. He'll never look at me as anything more than the guy who almost got his little girl killed."

I grind my teeth, annoyed with the entire conversation. "I know you think you know my dad, but you don't. Sure, he's protective…"

"Protective?" Pike laughs. "That man is way more than that."

"Let me finish," I growl, glaring at him. "The one thing I know about my family is that they know forgiveness. No one will judge you for things you didn't do or couldn't control. What went down wasn't your fault. My dad knows that. Deep down, he understands. He just needs some time to cool off and come to his right mind so he has a chance to figure it out for himself."

Pike shakes his head, throwing his arm over the steering wheel like we're out for a Sunday drive. "I know you have this need to be liked, babe, but I don't feel the same. I'm me. I can't change who I am. I can't change where I come from or what happened before I walked through the doors at Inked. If he doesn't like me, I'll be okay. It won't change how I feel about you."

I take a deep breath, letting his words settle before I dare open my mouth. My entire body is stiff, and being trapped in the truck, unable to move, isn't helping my anger either. "You think I can go through life with you and my father at each other's throats?" I gape at him.

Pike shrugs. "Don't know, but I guess we'll find out."

I run my hand down my face, groaning into my palm. "What a clusterfuck," I mutter. "I never should've let you talk to him about what happened."

"Nah, darlin'. I had to be the one to talk to him. I had to man up, and I did. He may not have liked what I said, but I said it. It's over. We're moving on."

I widen my eyes. "We're moving on, and it's over?"

What the fuck?

Pike nods, not looking at me as he keeps his gaze trained on the traffic in front of us.

"Are you fucking serious with that?" I ask, my voice all high-pitched and full of bitch.

"I can't control how your dad feels."

I close my eyes and whisper, "Fucker."

"I'm a fucker?"

I don't dare look at him. I'm too pissed to look at his face. I just stare straight ahead and snap, "Yep. Wake me if you want me to drive."

What the hell am I doing with someone like Pike? He's so much like my father, it's almost maddening sometimes. He's moody, difficult, and bossy. Nothing has been easy since the day he walked back into my life.

Daytona was easy. We were hundreds of miles away from everyone and everything. There weren't parents getting in our business or bad guys coming after us.

Pike's going through some shit. Some really dark shit. He's dealing with the death of his mother. He's about to face his past, including a little brother and grandmother he hasn't seen in years.

All I can do is be there for him and hope the guy I knew back in Daytona, the funny asshole who caught my eye, comes back to me.

I close my eyes, wanting nothing more than to get away from him for a little while. Since it's impossible, I do the next best thing. I go to sleep.

"We're here, darlin'." The backs of Pike's fingers brush against my cheek so softly I barely feel them.

I moan as I try to move. "Already?"

"Afraid so."

I blink a few times, trying to clear the haze from my mind. Gone is the endless gray of the road, replaced by an explosion of colors—lush green grass and a yellow-orange sky as the sun sets behind the mountains.

"Here they come." Pike dips his head toward the windshield as I stretch.

My gaze follows his to an older woman and young man as they walk out of a white house with a beautiful wraparound porch. I reach for the visor, pulling down the mirror to make sure I don't look as shitty as I feel.

"You're beautiful," Pike says as I wipe the mascara smeared under my eyes.

"You should've given me a heads-up," I whine in a panic.

"I tried, but you wouldn't wake up. Based on how fast Granny's walking, you still have a minute or two."

"Fuckin' men," I mutter, flipping up the visor, knowing my face is as good as it's going to get.

That is when I get my first real good look at his brother, Austin. He's a younger version of Pike, but with darker hair and no tattoos. He's holding his grandmother's arm, helping her down the walkway in front of her house like a little gentleman.

"Man," Pike says, taking in his granny and

brother. "I never realized how long I'd been gone until right now."

I reach across and grab his hand, locking our fingers together. Sure, he was a shithead, but I came here to support him, and support him I will.

"You ready for this?" I ask him, rubbing his wrist with my thumb.

"Don't have a choice." He shrugs.

"I'm here for you," I tell him, wishing we were here under happy circumstances.

There's a faint smile on his lips as he squeezes my fingers and reaches for the door handle with his other hand. "I wouldn't want anyone else by my side."

I slide out of the pickup truck, following Pike, and I hang back as he walks toward his grandmother.

Austin's gaze moves from Pike to me. When our eyes lock, a smug smirk plays on his lips before he throws me a wink like I'm going to kneel down at his feet and profess I've fallen for the wrong Moore.

Lordy.

I raise an eyebrow and stare at the kid. I mean, don't get me wrong, he's freakishly good-looking, but he's a baby.

"Granny, this is Gigi," Pike says, drawing my attention away from Austin.

I smile at the cute old woman with a bloom of white hair and soulful dark brown eyes. "It's an honor to meet you, ma'am," I declare with a big smile on my face, tucking a lock of hair behind my ear.

She steps forward, the wrinkles around her mouth deepening as she smiles. "Come closer, honey. I can't see so good with these old eyes." She motions for me, and I step forward, closing the space between us. I glance at Pike, who only gives me a nod.

She grabs my hands, holding them tightly, and peers into my eyes. "Such a natural beauty," she whispers. "I like a girl who doesn't have to put on a mountain of makeup to be seen."

I don't want to break the news to her that most of my face wore off somewhere between Florida and Tennessee. I've never worn a ton of makeup, but rarely do I leave the house this naked either.

"Thank you, ma'am."

"Connie, please." She pats my hand, making me feel welcome during such a difficult time.

"Connie," I repeat as Pike strides toward his brother, leaving us alone.

Connie doesn't let go of me as her gaze follows Pike, watching the brothers exchange words neither of us can hear. "My heart is happy now," Connie confesses, smiling at her grandsons. "It's nice to see them together. It's a shame it had to happen because of their mother's death."

"Yeah," I whisper back as they embrace each other for the first time in years.

"They need each other," she tells me. "Siblings are never complete when they're apart."

I get what she's saying. After I left home and headed off to college, I felt funny without my little sisters around. My entire life had been filled with them. I rarely had a moment alone, and then overnight, I had all the silence in the world.

"Maybe out of all this tragedy will come a bond stronger than they've ever had before. They really only have each other left," she says.

I turn my gaze toward Connie, our hands still connected. "They have you too."

"Honey, I'm an old woman. I don't have many days left on this earth, and it would give me peace knowing I'm not leaving them alone."

Sadness comes over me as she speaks. I don't often think about time. Death and dying are something I barely put any thought into. But standing with Connie, listening to her dreams for Pike and Austin, my mortality hits me square in the face.

"I'm sure the boys will get closer now that they're older," I reassure her, but who knows how Pike feels.

He's barely spoken about his brother. It's like they're strangers even though they spent years under the same roof. I couldn't imagine feeling the same way about my sisters.

"Let's give them some time together. Sweet tea?" she asks, pulling me gently toward the house.

They're so deep in conversation, neither of them notices as we walk away, leaving them alone. I hope whatever they're saying, they're finding a path back to each other.

"Please." I glance at Pike and Austin one last time before I follow her inside.

We're nothing without our family, and right now…they need each other.

4

PIKE

AUSTIN NEARLY COLLAPSES against me as soon as he's in my arms. "I'm so happy you're here," he whispers, holding on to me like I'm the only thing keeping him upright. "I feel so alone."

My heart aches for the first time since hearing about my mother's death. I'm not sad for the wicked woman, but I'm torn up for my little brother.

"I'm here for you." I hold him tighter, giving him the strength he needs.

"You don't know what it's been like." He pulls back, eyes glassy and swimming with tears. "No one knows."

He's no longer the little kid I'd left behind when I drove away from this small-ass town and the life I had here.

"I've missed you," he blurts out before I can reply.

I'm still soaking in the realization that my brother is a grown man and not a little boy anymore. "I've missed you too," I confess for the first time in my life.

My parents may have never treated me well, while they smothered Austin, but I never held any animosity toward the kid. He didn't rub it in my face or do anything to earn my hatred. That shit all fell on my parents. He was the only one in the house who was nice to me and paid me any attention, which I know drove my parents crazy.

"Stick around for a few days, yeah?"

I nod, unable to find my voice as the guilt of all the years I've missed washes over me. All the moments I wasn't here for him. All the milestones I didn't get to see. Memories I should've been a part of but wasn't and never will be.

"You look…" Austin's voice trails off as he rocks back on his heels.

I raise an eyebrow with a small smirk, hoping to lighten the dark mood. "Like shit?"

He runs his fingers through his dark hair, glancing down at his feet to hide his smile. "Your words, not mine."

There's an awkward pause. I'm not sure what to say after so many years, and I'm pretty sure he feels the same.

I glance toward the patio where Gigi and Granny just were, but they're gone. "Life has a way of wearing on our skin. You'll learn that as you grow older."

"If that were true, I'd look like an old piece of leather." He grimaces. "I ain't ready for all that."

"You're only seventeen, Aus. Your skin's too new to show the wreckage." I knock him on the shoulder, trying to be playful even when it's not the time.

"Thirsty?" he asks, finding his footing and straightening his back.

I nod. "I could use something to drink."

"Granny grabbed a six-pack from the corner store, but she said I can't have one." He rolls his blue eyes, rubbing the back of his neck. "She's absolutely no fun, brother."

"You don't need fun in your life right now. Fun around here means bad shit and even worse people." I point my finger at him. "The last thing you need is that kind of *fun.*"

Austin smacks my finger away and throws his arm around my shoulder. "A drink with my brother isn't the bad type of fun. I just want to kick back, shoot the shit over a beer, and find out where the hell you've been for the last ten years."

"You don't want to know," I argue.

"Sure I do. You just disappeared. Poof. Gone."

I wince as more guilt floods my belly.

He turns his head, giving me his eyes, and I brace myself for his next words. "It was like you were the one who died, but you were alive, forgetting all about me."

The confirmation I'd abandoned him cuts me deep. I had never put much thought into how my leaving town would affect him. He was seven when I left, and I didn't think he'd even notice.

I mean, we barely saw each other. At least not like most siblings. My parents made sure of that. They did everything to keep us apart from the day I moved in with Granny.

"Let's get that beer and go down by the river, yeah?" I ask him, figuring Granny won't put up too much of a stink.

"You get the beer, and I'll meet you down at the spot?" He moves his head toward the path still cut in the thick brush lining the driveway. "It'll be easier," he says as his hand falls away from my shoulder.

"Be there in five," I tell him before he disappears into the woods, and I go into the house. Nothing has changed since the last time I was here. It's like time stood still in this place, while I moved on with my life.

"Where's Austin?" Granny asks, leaning over the kitchen island where two glasses of sweet tea sit in front of them.

"He's down by the river, waiting on me," I say, glancing at my girl, who looks comfortable sitting in my granny's kitchen.

Granny raises an eyebrow, knowing exactly what

happens down by the river. "He's only seventeen, Pike."

I shrug before walking behind Gigi and putting my arms around her shoulders. "I'm pretty sure it's not going to be the first beer he's ever had."

Gigi glances over her shoulder at me, grabbing on to my hands. "Don't drink too much, okay?"

I kiss the top of Gigi's head as Granny eyes me. "I won't. Just a few, darlin'. We'll be back before you know it. Are you okay staying here with her?" I ask Gigi.

Granny crosses her arms, tilting her head and narrowing her eyes. "I'm a *her* now?"

I laugh. "Granny, I know how you are. I just want to make sure you're being good to my girl."

She shakes her head and wrinkles her nose. "She's the first woman you've ever brought home. You can bet your ass I'm going to be on my best behavior, but that doesn't mean I'm not going to have some questions about my grandson or the beautiful girl in my kitchen." Her lips slide into a smile. "We'll be fine. I promise."

"Just go," Gigi agrees, trying to hold back her giggles at the ridiculousness of the conversation. "I think your granny and I will get along perfectly, babe."

"We're just going to have a little girl time. You

need to go have some boy time with Austin," Granny tells me, leveling me with her gaze.

"We're hardly boys," I correct her, "but we do need to have a man-to-man talk." I kiss Gigi's cheek before heading toward the fridge. I open the doors to the mostly empty refrigerator and grab the six-pack, turning to find both women studying me in sheer fascination. "What?"

Granny smiles. "It's just nice to see you here again. Go be with Austin. Don't come back until later. We'll get dinner started."

"What the hell are you going to make?" I pitch a thumb over my shoulder toward the empty fridge. "There's nothing in there."

"Pike, I've made more with less. Now, go." Granny shoos me toward the door.

It's a short walk to the river's edge where Austin's sitting in an old Adirondack chair. He's hunched over, elbows on his knees, holding a stick in one hand, smacking the water with the tip.

"Sorry I took so long." I set the six-pack between us and sit in the lawn chair next to him. "The girls…"

"Did you call Granny a girl to her face?" Austin asks.

I shrug, laughing because he knows as well as I do how much she hates it. "Maybe." I reach for two beers and offer him one. "She can try to beat my ass now, but I'm a little too big and too fast."

Austin laughs too, taking the beer from my hand. "She's too old for all that. Now she just gives you the look when you've fucked up. You know the look?"

I nod, knowing damn well the way she can put the fear of death in you with just a single squint and crook of her lips.

"I get it a lot," he says, twisting the top off the beer before throwing the cap in the mud. "She's slower now but still scary."

I kick back, relaxing in a spot where I spent a lot of time during my childhood. "Granny's all bark and no bite. I couldn't say the same for some people in our lives."

Austin grimaces. He is young, but he wasn't blind. "I don't know why they were always so good to me and treated you like shit." Pain flashes in his eyes. "I'm sorry."

"You didn't do anything wrong. Don't even think about it, Aus. We all go through shit in life. That was mine to deal with. I've moved past everything. I got away and landed places where people wanted me. I may have been born into the family by blood, but I found my new family by choice."

He looks off into the distance as he rests the bottle on his leg. "Where did you go?"

I follow his eyes, ogling the same patch of trees. There has been pain for both of us. Mine was caused by the people he loved the most, and his was by my absence and our mother's death.

"I just took off," I confess softly, digging the heels of my boots into the thick mud near the shore. "I wanted to be anywhere but here."

He glances at me, eyebrows drawn inward. "And went where?"

"I headed south." I shrug, wondering how much I should tell him. But then I figure, I shouldn't hold anything back. "I left with five hundred bucks in my pocket. Slept in some pretty shady motels as I made my way to Florida, blowing through most of my cash before I hit the Georgia-Florida line."

He turns in his chair, giving me his full attention. Attention I don't really want but have no choice but to take. "Then what did you do?"

"My life took an unexpected turn near Jacksonville."

He raises his eyebrows. "Jacksonville?"

"Yeah. I was minding my own business, filling my bike's tank with some gas, when all hell broke loose."

"What happened?"

"Got my ass shot that night," I say, smiling as I think back on the stupidity of the entire thing.

His eyes widen as soon as the words are out of my mouth. "Shot?" he gasps.

"Some bikers had a beef with some jackasses nearby. I got caught in the cross fire."

"Jesus," he mutters, shaking his head. "Where did you get shot?"

"My shoulder." I rub the spot where I'll always have a scar. "It wasn't too bad, but I was pissed. I got into it with one of the guys, and he ended up punching me in the shoulder, making me kiss the cement."

"What the fuck?" Austin's mouth hangs open. "For real? The asshole punched you in your wound?"

I nod, knowing how fucked up it sounds. "I passed out from the pain after that. I don't remember anything until I woke up at their compound."

Austin swallows as his knuckles turn white from gripping his beer so tightly. "Were you scared?"

I shake my head, lying my ass off because if you aren't a little scared in a situation like that, then you're really a dumbass. "Well, I wasn't happy when I woke up. My shoulder was fixed and the bullet removed, but I had no idea what they had planned for me. When I saw the guy who punched me, it took three men to hold me back from getting my retribution." I chuckle, remembering the shock on Morris's face when I lunged at him.

Austin gives me a cocky smile. "I would've punched that fucker square in his jaw. He'd be eating nothing but smoothies for a month."

I laugh at my brother's greenness. If he knew Morris, ever laid eyes on the man, he'd realize there was no way he'd have the kind of power to actually break his jaw. "I never did get to give him payback, but after I talked with him, I understood why he did it."

"I don't think I could ever get over something like that," he mutters.

I throw back half the beer, letting the cool liquid coat my throat, trying to come up with some words of wisdom. "As you grow older, you realize some things aren't worth holding grudges over. At some point, you've just got to move on, or else you'll always be stuck looking back."

Austin leans back in his chair, eyes going back to the forest with the sun cascading through the leaves. "I guess so," he whispers. "What happened after that?"

I let out a sigh, knowing there's so much to the story. I could talk about my time with the Disciples for days and never really get into everything that happened. "They invited me to stay after they found out I had nowhere to go. I ended up living there for a few years, hanging out with the guys, feeling like I was part of a family for the first time in my life."

The only family I'd ever known.

"Wait." He slices his eyes to mine. "You lived with a biker gang?"

I nod, lifting my beer to my lips and pausing. "Only for a little while."

"You said a few years," he corrects me, throwing my own words back in my face.

I shrug. "That's a little while. As you get older, years aren't as long. It went by in the blink of an eye."

"Did you go on runs and kill people too?" he asks.

I shake my head. "Never. I never prospected with them. Never wanted to be in a biker club. They gave me a place to live and I did some stuff for them to pay my way, but damn, it wasn't as bad as you're making it sound. You watch way too much television."

"*Sons of Anarchy* was my favorite show, dude. Now I find out I have my very own Jax Teller in the family."

I bark out a laugh at his statement. "Austin, I am not and have never been Jax Teller. I wasn't in the Disciples. I didn't wear their cut. I was like the live-in help. They gave me a room, food, and let me hang around, but that's about it."

"They have all those wild parties?" He raises an eyebrow because he's seventeen and probably thinks about sex as often as he breathes.

"No," I lie and try to keep my face as neutral as possible.

"Liar." He rolls his eyes. "You're telling me they don't have half-naked women all around their compound?"

"If they did, I never saw it." That is my story, and I am sticking to it. In no way do I want to make the life sound even a little bit like something a horny teenage boy would enjoy.

"Whatever," he mumbles against the top of the beer bottle. "How long did you stay with them?"

"A few years, honing my skills as a tattoo artist. I loved to draw. It was always my thing. My escape. But drawing in a book and doing it on flesh are two different things."

"I remember you always sketching something or other."

"The guys in the club let me use them as my guinea pigs. They got free tattoos until I was pretty fucking good at it."

"So, you got room and board, and they got free tattoos?" he asks, repeating my statement.

"Something like that," I say.

"It was a nice trade-off. Plus, I'm sure the tits and ass were a bonus too." He laughs, knowing I'm full of shit.

I'm going to go right on by that because he doesn't need to know about all the tits and ass.

God, there was so much, too. All shapes, sizes, ages. Thirsty bitches who wanted nothing more than to fuck and suck their way through the members of the club.

I was young and didn't care about anything else except for getting off. I wasn't looking for long-term. I wanted casual, and the ladies around the club were perfect for something like that.

"I never really had much trouble getting tits and ass, kid." I wink at him. "That's one thing Mom and Dad gave us…good genes. We're damn good-lookin'."

"I don't know about your ugly mug, but I'm fucking hot." He touches his chest, giving me a smug grin. "Ask any of the chicks around here. They're all chomping to get a piece of me."

I roll my eyes, remembering when I was just as cocky as he is now. That's youth. Life has a way of reminding you you're not as great as you think you are. "Tell me what you really think of yourself." I laugh at my little brother as he kisses his bicep.

"Nah. I'm sure you can see the perfectness that's me. Now, I want to know what happened and why you left the Disciples."

I slam back the last of my beer and reach for another one. Eventually, we're going to get off of me and move on to the shit that went down after I left.

"It was just time to go. I headed out after tattooing at a local shop for about a year, moving a few hours south where I could find a chair. I still saw the guys, caught up with them every year at Bike Week in Daytona, but I had my sights set on bigger and better things than anything I could get with the Disciples."

"So, you're living somewhere south of Jacksonville?"

I shake my head. "I live north of Tampa now."

His eyebrows furrow. "What? How?"

"So, I lived near Daytona for a while, doing tats in a decent shop, but I wanted to work at the best shop in Florida. They were always in every tattoo magazine, featured for their killer work and designs. I wanted to work there from the day I put my first mark on someone's skin."

"And they're in Tampa?"

"They're about an hour north. Middle of fucking nowhere, but not like here. There's still civilization around, but it's a quieter way of life than Daytona with all the tourist bullshit."

"And the hot chick?" He tips his head toward the path leading back to Granny's. "How does she fit in?"

"I met her in Daytona, but her family owns Inked. She works there, and now I work there too."

"No shit. You're fucking the boss's daughter." His mouth hangs open.

"Watch it. That's my girl you're talking about."

"Well…" He turns the beer in his hand, swiping at the water drops with his thumb. "You are sleeping with her, yeah? She's not just a friend who tagged along?"

"She's my girlfriend, yeah."

"So, after all this time, you found what you were

looking for? You achieved your dream, and the girl is the bonus."

"She's the real dream," I confess as my throat grows tight. "But I didn't know that when I walked into Inked. I thought I'd achieved everything I'd ever wanted when I got my spot. But Gigi…" I shake my head, unable to stop myself from smiling. "That girl and her family, they're really what I've always wanted. Just never knew it until it landed in my lap."

Austin kicks at the dirt near his feet, setting down the empty bottle before grabbing another. "You do have a family here, you know," he heckles, flicking his eyes at me.

"I've never forgotten about you and Granny. Time has a way of getting away from someone. And…" I pause, running my hand down the front of my jeans. "I figured it was easier for everyone if I just disappeared."

He narrows his eyes. "Easier for who?"

I blink, at a loss for words.

"You or us?" he adds.

It's like he's punched me square in the chest without even lifting a finger. The words sting. "I guess, for me," I answer honestly.

Austin leans forward, resting his elbows on his knees, casting his eyes downward. "I needed you. I wanted you here. I was only seven when you left, but I used to love coming to see you." His eyes flicker to mine. "I didn't care what Mom and Dad said, you were and are my brother. I still remember when I walked into her house and Granny told me you were gone." He shakes his head, blowing out a long breath. "It was like someone kicked me in the face."

"I'm sorry." I rub my forehead, wincing as his words connect with every emotion I've shoved down so deep I never let myself feel any of them. "I was a shit brother for leaving without saying goodbye."

"You *are* a shit brother." He drives that knife in a little deeper and twists.

I study his dark brown hair, wide build, athletic body, all of which look nothing like mine. "I hope to change that. I need to make amends for the time we lost."

"You do." He doesn't even flinch when he says those words. "It sucks that Mom dying was the reason you finally came home, but I'm happy you're here."

"I'm sorry about Mom." I rest my head against the back of the chair, watching the clouds passing over us. "She and I had a complicated relationship, but I never would've wanted this for her or you."

"I was there," Austin confesses, drawing my gaze. "No one knows. Not even Granny."

My body stiffens. "You were where?"

"In the house," he says quietly.

Jesus. "When she died?"

He nods slowly, his lower lip trembling. "We both

hid. She told me not to come out, no matter what happened. They found me first and used me to lure her into the open."

"They found you?" I gape at my brother, trying to imagine the sheer terror he had to have felt.

He nods again, frown firmly planted on his face. "I was hiding in the closet, and they dragged me out. I tried to fight them off, but I was outnumbered. I told them she wasn't there. I told them I was alone, but they didn't believe me." He slumps forward and sighs.

"Fuck," I hiss, wishing I could take the memories away from him.

"They punched me in the face before kicking my feet out from under me. They held a gun to my head in the middle of the living room and waited, knowing Mom would eventually come out."

I shake my head, imagining the entire situation. The scared seventeen-year-old boy with a gun to his head, and a mother who adored him, lured into the open.

Sickening.

"It only took a few minutes, but she came downstairs, pleading with them to let me go." He turns his head away and wipes at his face with the back of his hand. "I think they hit me with the butt of the gun. I was knocked out cold. I didn't see what happened, but when I woke up..." He pauses and swallows, his Adam's apple moving like it's fighting an unwinnable battle. "Mom was lying in a pool of blood with the back of her head missing." He goes back to staring at the trees, trying to be nothing but strong at a time when I'd be falling apart.

"Jesus fucking Christ," I mutter and take a deep breath. "I'm sorry for all of it. For you having to find Mom like that. For having to go through the entire thing alone."

"Maybe now that you're here…" He looks at me with so much hope in his eyes, my heart aches. "I'll never have to go through something like that by myself again."

"Yeah," I reply, knowing it's a promise I can't keep.

5

PIKE

Gigi's boots come into view as I sit on the porch, trying to digest everything Austin told me. "What are you going to do about Austin?" she asks.

I lift my gaze, traveling slowly up her bare legs to her cute little tank top and finally landing on her face. "What do you mean, what am I going to do about Austin?"

She crosses her arms and furrows her brows like we're speaking two different languages. "After this. What's going to happen to him?"

What's going to happen to him? I haven't put much thought into where my brother will go after the funeral is over. "I figured he'd stay here."

Gigi's face morphs into something unreadable. "You know your grandmother is getting older, yeah?"

"I'm not blind."

"Maybe she doesn't want to raise another child at her age," she tells me.

"Child?" I laugh as I lean back in the chair. "He's seventeen. He's hardly a kid, and in a year, he'll go off to college or wherever the hell else he wants to go."

"Pike," she says, shaking her head like I've just said the most insane thing in the world.

"Gigi."

"He can't stay here."

I jerk my head back. "He can't? I stayed here, and I turned out just fine."

"Nope," she says bluntly, tapping her foot, clearly pissed off at me…again. "Your grandmother cannot control a seventeen-year-old boy who's going through some shit after losing his mother. Someone needs to watch out for him so he doesn't end up surrounded by bad people. Imagine if you were a different type of man and got involved with the MC. Where would you be now?"

I put my hands behind my head, trying to keep calm while she grows angrier. "No one can control someone else. If he's going to fuck up his life, he'll do it whether he stays here or goes somewhere else." I shrug off her comment.

"He won't fuck it up if someone guides him."

"He's grown now."

She moves her hands to her hips, and I know she's gearing up for a fight. "He's a kid."

"If he hasn't learned how to act or stay out of trouble by seventeen, there's no help for him anyway, Gigi."

Taking Austin with me and being responsible for someone other than myself scares the shit out of me.

She blows out a shaky breath. "I can't believe I'm hearing this from you."

"What the fuck do you want me to do?" I growl, but I know what she's saying isn't totally off base.

"You're a coldhearted bastard sometimes." She's trying to run my life, something I've seen all the Gallos do to one another on a daily basis. "You should take him home," she says finally, getting to her point.

I shake my head, thinking I had to have heard her wrong. "Say that again."

She leans her ass against the railing and sighs. "It doesn't make sense for him to stay here. He needs you right now. You have a place, a stable job, and although sometimes you're a dick, you're basically a good guy."

"Thanks for the compliment," I mutter.

"Shut up," she growls. "Why would you leave him here?"

"She's right," Granny says from the door, hiding behind the screen and eavesdropping like she always used to do.

"Fuck," I groan. They're going to double-team me.

"Now, Pike," Granny says, sitting down in the rocking chair next to me. "Your girlfriend—" she dips her head toward Gigi, who is standing there with a smug grin "—is bringing up a valid point about Austin."

I rub my forehead, readying myself for the assault from two sides. I never imagined my grandma would want Austin to come live with me. Never in a million freaking years.

Hell, we barely know each other.

The kid liked toy trucks the last time he and I breathed the same air, and now he's driving a real one.

"You can't seriously think it's a good idea?" I scoff.

Granny nods, giving me a sweet smile, which always made me crumble in the past. "He needs guidance."

I lean forward again, resting my elbows on my knees, scanning the wood planks beneath my feet. "I can barely guide myself, Granny. I don't think Austin coming to live with me would be a good idea."

No fucking way am I taking this kid home with me.

"Your daddy's in jail, and your mama's in her casket. He needs a man in his life to show him the way. He needs to know how to survive in this crazy world I don't understand. I'm old, Pike. Too old to be raising a teenager." Granny takes a long sip of her tea, giving me time to process what she's just said.

I study Gigi as she glances down at her feet, avoiding my eyes completely as Granny continues.

"If Austin were a girl, I would keep her. Show her how to be a lady and not put up with any boy's shit, but he isn't. Lord knows your father didn't teach him how to be a man. That leaves you, and I know what kind of man you are."

Without my granny, I'm not sure where I'd be or, hell, who I'd be. No matter what I was doing, I always wondered about the possibility of disappointing her, and that single thought stopped me from doing some stupid shit in the last ten years.

"No. It's not happening," I tell her, standing from the chair. "This conversation is over."

"We'll see," Granny brags, but I don't turn around to see her smug smile.

Fuck my life.

6

PIKE

"Will you come in with me?" Austin asks me as we stand in the hallway of the funeral home.

Gigi squeezes my hand, silently pleading with me not to be an asshole. "Sure," I tell him, making my girl happy, but me miserable at the same time.

The last thing I want is time alone with the woman who made me feel like nothing but garbage for most of my childhood.

Do I wish she were alive? Sure.

I'd never wish death on someone unless they were trying to kill me or mine. But am I torn up over her taking her last breath?

Not in the least.

Austin brushes his hand across his dark hair, making sure it's perfect for the tenth time since we walked through the door. He looks ten years older in his black suit and nothing like the kid I left behind.

Gigi pops up on her tiptoes, brushing her lips across my cheek. “Be there for him,” she whispers. “He needs you.”

I peer down into her blue eyes. “I will,” I reassure her, speaking softly so no one else can hear.

Granny turns toward Austin, playing with his tie to make sure it’s perfect just like his hair. “It’s okay to cry,” she tells him as he lifts his head.

“I’m not going to cry, Gran.”

She touches his face with her fingertips and gives him a pained smile. “I know you’re grown, Austin, but it’s okay to feel things.”

He grabs her wrist, gently pulling her hand away from his cheek. “I’ll be okay.”

I release Gigi and straighten my jacket for whatever fucking reason. I hold my breath as the funeral director moves in front of the double doors.

“Please let me know if you’re unhappy with anything,” he declares solemnly.

If we’re unhappy with anything?

Is anyone ever happy at a funeral?

“We will, sir,” Austin tells him, sounding very much like an adult.

Austin keeps surprising me. He’s handled the man with grace and respect, something I couldn’t do, and I’m not even torn up about being here. He not only looks older than he is, but he acts like it at times too. Sure, there're still remnants of the little boy there, but he's seen things I can't imagine.

He found her.

I take a deep breath, following behind my brother as we step into the room filled with wooden chairs placed in neat, even rows. In the front, surrounded by flowers, is a white casket, half open and with my mother's face clearly visible.

Austin freezes, his shoulders going rigid. "I don't know if I can do this." His back is to me, and his gaze is firmly locked on our mother.

I step next to him, placing my hand on his shoulder. "I'll be right here with you."

Austin sucks in a deep breath, closing his eyes for a moment and muttering something so quietly I can't make out the words. When he exhales, he opens his eyes and looks over his shoulder at me. "I don't think I could've done this without you, big brother."

Every time he calls me brother, the guilt of leaving him grows roots, settling in my bones.

I wish I could go back.

Change the way I left things. I should've kept in contact with him. It wouldn't have changed where we are standing, but it would've made my presence mean more than it actually did.

When he doesn't move, I squeeze his shoulder again. "I won't leave you," I promise him.

"I'll hold you to that." He takes a step, moving out of my grasp.

I follow behind, my eyes going back to our mother's motionless body.

Austin's steps are long and slow as he closes the gap between himself and Augusta Moore.

High-class socialite.

Piss-poor mother.

His knees buckle as soon as he's within a few feet of her, landing on the tiny kneeling bench in front of her. His hands shake as he places them on the edge of the casket. "Fuck," he hisses, brushing the backs of his fingers across his face, no doubt wiping away tears he said he wouldn't shed.

I slide into a chair in the first row, careful to give him space to feel what he needs to feel.

I face forward, the words *Loving Mother* nestled in a flower arrangement resting on the lid catching my attention.

Now that's laughable.

"She looks so good." He turns his face. "Don't you think?"

I look at her, trying to make Austin happy, and I finally see my mother's face clearly for the first time in years. "Yeah." My throat starts to close as the realization that the woman who gave birth to me is gone. Dead.

My mind buzzes with so many things.

So many fucked-up emotions I didn't expect to have wash over me, coating me like a second skin.

Sadness.

Remorse.

Longing.

Regret.

"Just remember, baby. I'll always love you," she says as she slides my favorite pajamas over my head. "Never think otherwise."

I throw my arms around her neck as soon as she starts to pull away, planting a wet kiss against her cheek. "I love you too, Mommy," I whisper against her soft skin. "Forever and always."

"Forever and always." She wraps her arms around me tightly, nestling her face against my neck, tickling me. "Now, crawl into bed, and I'll read you a story."

I practically leap out of her grasp, climbing up on my cool race car bed, tucking myself under the covers. "I want the baseball book." I smile up at her as she walks toward my nightstand, the book I want already waiting.

She sits down, tapping my nose with her thin finger, giving me a big smile. "As if any other book exists."

I giggle because I love this part of the day.

It's only her and me.

No Dad because he's been extra grouchy, ignoring me more than usual.

But Mom…she makes me happy.

I reach for my neck, loosening the tie, suddenly

unable to breathe. How could a woman so loving turn on a dime?

"Who's Ashton?" my father asks Mom as she reaches for the coffeepot.

I look up because my father's voice is angrier than usual. The toy truck in my hand is in midair, and I can't stop myself from staring at my mother as she stands so still, it's like she's frozen.

"Ashton?" she whispers, giving my father a funny look.

My father steps behind her, holding up a piece of paper and shaking it in her face. "Don't play stupid with me, Augusta. I already know, but I want to hear it from your lying, cheating lips."

I widen my eyes when he reaches for her, wrapping his hands around her arms, forcing her to face him. Although Dad's not nice, he's never laid his hands on her before.

"Colton, you're hurting me." She glances down at his hand and winces. "I have no idea who Ashton is."

Dad's face grows redder, and his jaw pulses, the same way it does when he's about to lay into me for being a pest. "Do you know what this is?" He shakes the piece of paper in her face again.

She stares him straight in the eyes, not even bothering to look at the white sheet. "No."

"I knew that bastard wasn't mine. Had the DNA test to prove it two years ago, but could never figure out who you fucked"—he says that word so loud, she flinches—"until now."

I stand quickly, dropping my toy truck to the carpet, and

run toward the kitchen. "You let go of her!" I shout, grabbing at my dad's arm.

His angry gaze slices to me, his teeth showing with his lips curled. "Get the hell away, little asshole." He pushes me with his elbow.

I topple backward, catching myself with my hands before my butt hits the floor. "Don't you touch her!" I yell, climbing to my feet to rescue her.

I have to.

His foot is in the air, connecting with my stomach before I have a chance to straighten. I fly back, my ass landing hard on the tile floor as I gasp for air and tears fill my eyes.

"Don't," she pleads. "I'll tell you whatever you want to know. Just leave him alone."

Tears trickle down my cheeks as I curl into a ball, trying to catch my breath.

No one comes to my rescue.

No one seems to care, not even my mom, that I can't breathe.

"Who is he?"

"He doesn't live here anymore."

"Augusta, so help me God." He raises his hand again, and she flinches.

"He used to deliver our mail."

My father's eyes narrow, and his entire body rocks back like he's the one who's been hit. "You fucked the mailman?"

My mother smirks, holding his angry glare. "Many times," she taunts him. "So, so many times."

"The boy that has my name is the fucking mailman's kid?"

My mother's smirk breaks into a wide smile. "He is."

"And this one?" My father's eyes fall down to her stomach, where my little brother's growing.

"He's yours."

My father wraps his fingers around her neck, and her face turns red. "If I find out this one isn't mine, Augusta…"

Tears trickle down her cheeks. "Please," she gasps, clawing at his fingers. "I can't breathe."

"That one," he snarls, turning toward me, "is nothing. Not to me. Not to you. He's nothing. Do you hear me?"

"He's…"

"He's what?" my father challenges.

"He's my baby."

"He's nothing to you. If you want to keep either of the children, he's nothing to either of us."

I wipe at my face, sniffling as my nose starts to run.

I'm not nothing.

I'm their little boy.

I'm the one Mommy loves the most.

My father moves his head so close to hers, their noses are touching. "So help me God, if you want to keep breathing and for your bastard to live too, you'll do as I say."

"But I can't…"

"You will!" he shouts.

She nods as her eyes find me for a brief moment, and I think everything's going to be okay.

But then he shakes her body, lifting her off the floor by her throat. "I'm not playing with you, Augusta. Don't test me."

Her eyes leave me, and her gaze goes blank. "I swear, Colton," she gasps.

He places her feet back on the floor and releases her neck. "Traitorous bitch," he mumbles and turns to face me. "Nothing but a no-good bastard."

I'm a good boy. I always follow the rules and listen to Mommy, careful not to upset my dad. Today, I did nothing wrong, yet he looks angrier with me than he ever has before.

"Mommy," I whisper, lifting my arms, looking for her embrace.

She steps forward, and I smile, thinking she's going to wipe away my sadness and give me the snuggles she's always been so good at giving.

She doesn't reach out for me.

She doesn't even look at me.

She steps forward, grabbing the piece of paper he'd dropped on the floor, and walks out of the room.

"Pike?" Austin whispers.

I sit there unable to move, memories I'd locked down so deep flooding back.

Colton Moore isn't my father.

The news I'd long forgotten crashes over me, leaving me with more questions than answers. I'll never be able to find out why or how. How could she turn her back on me so easily? Sure, she was trying to protect me, but she could've gotten away from Colton and made a new home for us. She could've done anything more than she did.

"Yeah?" I blink, chasing away the tears filling my eyes.

He studies my face, still kneeling in front of our mother's casket. "You okay?"

I nod, not trusting my voice.

"You want to say anything to Mom?"

More than you want to hear.

"Kneel with me," he pleads, motioning toward his side. "I want you here with me."

Austin's the only person besides my grandmother who ever made me feel wanted in my family. He looked up to me from the time he could talk, always trying to get me to play cars when I was too busy being pissed off at the world.

I move to be at his side because my kid brother deserves my attention.

Austin grasps my hand as soon as I'm next to him. "She wasn't an awful mom all the time, Pike," he comments like he's reading my mind. "Was she?"

I shake my head, choking back the suffocating sadness. "Not always, kid."

I'd blocked out anything good we'd ever had before walking into this room. It was easier never to think about the happy times, the moments where I felt loved, before my father took it all away.

She allowed it to happen.

She didn't fight back.

She didn't try to run.

She gave up on me.

He squeezes my fingers as I take in our mother's pale, serene face. "She loved you, you know."

"I don't know, Aus. It doesn't feel like she ever did."

"She told me," he whispers, even though we're alone. "Sometimes, when Dad wasn't around, she'd talk about you."

My entire body jerks back. "Austin, you don't have to lie to make me feel better. I'm a big guy, and I know exactly how she felt."

He shakes his head, eyes dark and serious but still swimming with tears. "I remember how she treated you, Pike. I was there. I was little, but I saw." He bows his head and gives it a slight shake. "It wasn't right, and I'll never understand why. But sometimes, she'd talk about you like you were everything in the world to her."

"You were everything to her, Austin. Mom adored you. Dad too."

"I'll miss her," he admits sadly. "No one will ever love me as much as she did."

I wish I could say the same, but I can't. I miss the version of my mother that was tucked so deep in my memory, it took seeing her dead body for me to remember.

She's the one I'll miss.

But this shell…the awful woman who turned her back on me, I won't give her a second thought.

"I love you, Austin." I look over at him, placing my hand on top of his. "I'll always love you. I can't replace Mom, but I want you to know you're not alone."

He gives me a halfhearted smile, pulling my hand in front of his and placing them both against the casket. "If she did nothing else right in her life, she gave us each other."

"I'm so sorry for your loss," Mrs. Daniels, my high school English teacher, declares as she shakes my hand. "She was a lovely woman."

"Thank you," I repeat for what feels like the hundredth time this afternoon. I'm on autopilot, and my voice is robotic.

"Mrs. D," Austin greets her from my side, taking her hand as soon as she offers it to him.

I take a deep, shaky breath when Gigi grasps my hand. "You're doing great, baby. Just another hour."

I smile at the next person, Mr. Porter, the town butcher. "The town has a hole in it now that your mother's gone, son."

I shake his hand, giving him a fake smile because

he must've known a different woman than I did. "Thank you," I repeat.

"She was so selfless and kind."

Augusta Moore was neither selfless nor kind. At least, not to me. But the people of this town see her differently. And no matter how hard I try, I can't wrap my head around any of their compliments.

"I'm sure someone will step into her shoes easily enough, Mr. Porter."

The creases in his forehead deepen as he bristles. "Son, your mother was the biggest donor for our feed the homeless program. She had an especially soft spot for the children, and I don't know how we're going to feed them all without her generosity."

Wait. Hold up.

My mom cared about homeless kids? Everyone in this small town thinks of my mother as a saint. She somehow became the Mother Teresa of Tennessee after I left.

The funeral is supposed to be my closure, but I'm walking away with more questions than I had before.

7

PIKE

"ARE YOU LEAVING TODAY?" Gran asks as she pours herself a cup of coffee.

"We are."

We're alone. Gigi and Austin are still sleeping, and the sun hasn't even kissed the sky. I didn't sleep at all last night. There was too much on my mind to find even a minute's peace.

Gran walks over to the table, setting down her cup across from me before sitting. "You takin' Austin with you?"

I turn my coffee cup in a circle, wrestling with that same question I've been asking myself all night. "I think so."

"There's no thinking involved, Pike." Granny studies me across the table, tapping her long fingernail against the rim of her mug. "You either are or you aren't. You know that's the right thing to do in your heart."

"Do you know about Ashton?"

Gran sucks in a breath. "That's a name I haven't heard in a while."

"So, you know." I glance down, realizing the only grandmother I've ever had isn't even mine, but she knew.

She knew.

"Baby," she sighs softly, reaching across the table and placing her hand on mine. "Get that thought right out of your head."

I look up, that fullness I felt in my throat yesterday back and stronger than ever.

"You're every bit as much my family as Austin is. You and I have a bond. A bond I've never shared or felt for anyone else except you."

"How long have you known?" I whisper.

She glances down and blinks. "Since you were a little boy. Maybe about six. When I found out about her affair, your mother was pregnant with the baby she lost."

"How do I not remember her losing a baby?"

Granny pats my hand, giving me a sad smile. "You came to stay with me for the week. I told you they went on vacation."

I turn to the window, gazing across the empty pasture. "I remember that."

So much of my childhood is a blur. It's like I blocked everything out, jumbling up events to protect myself from the hurt and anger. There are years missing, events just gone from my memory.

"Your mother would never admit it, but I'm pretty sure your father…" She pauses and grimaces. "I mean, Colton—had something to do with her losing that baby."

"I don't remember, Gran, but I know he'd laid his hands on her before. I saw it with my own eyes."

She shakes her head, twisting her lips as she bows her head. "I don't know how I raised such a rotten bastard."

I reach out, wrapping my fingers around her hand, and wait for her to look at me again. "You did everything you could. You are loving and kind. Sometimes, men are born bad, and no matter what you do, you can't make them into something they're never meant to be."

"You're a wise one, child. Always so wise for your years. You were forced to grow up before you should've. I should've fought harder to bring you home with me. You know I tried for years. Colton had a fit every time I brought it up. But as you got bigger, he knew he couldn't control you anymore, and only then did he allow me to take you. I wanted you. I wanted to love you like you should've been loved by your parents."

"I'll forever be grateful to you for giving me a home, Gran."

"That's what family does, Pike. Or at least, what they're supposed to do." She reaches into the pocket of her robe, fishing out an envelope and sliding the paper across the table. "I was holding this for the right time and I don't think it'll ever come, but this is as close as I'll get." She taps on the front where my name is written in my mother's handwriting. "Your mother asked me to give this to you if anything ever happened to her. I hope it gives you some peace."

Her hand disappears from the envelope, and she gets up, walking away from the table.

"Gran," I call out, wishing she'd stay.

"Read it, Pike. I'll be on the porch when you're done," she commands without even looking back.

When I flip the envelope over, I can see the back has been torn open. No doubt, Gran already read every word before she decided to give it to me.

I pull out the single sheet of folded paper, my mother's fancy, loopy cursive covering both sides. I unfold the sheet, hold my breath, and start to read.

My Dearest Pike,

I'm sorry.

It's such a simple statement. I wish I had the chance to say these words to your face, but they still need to be said. I was an awful mother and an even worse person for turning my back on you.

I should've been stronger.

I should've fought harder.

For you.

For me.

For us.

I was a coward, too fearful of Colton and too scared to try to run away. A man like him would stop at nothing to find us, making every nightmare I dreamed come true.

Your happiness was the casualty.

The love you deserved was stripped from you, making you shoulder the guilt and blame like you'd done something wrong. I saw the change in you over time.

The hurt.

The anger.

The loneliness you endured due to my fateful decisions.

I love you, son.

I loved you more than you'll ever understand or believe.

The regret I carry with me every day gnaws at my insides, staying with me like an invisible scar.

Colton took one child from me, but I wouldn't let him take you and Austin too.

For that, you were the victim, but I did what I needed to do to keep you alive, hoping I could make amends someday.

As the years passed, you grew distant and hateful, rightfully so. By then, I knew my words would seem hollow, and I left you alone, figuring your hate would be easier for you than the truth.

Colton Moore is not your father.

While you carry his name, you share no blood with the vile man who threatened my children so long ago.

Your father is Ashton Miller, a kind, joyful man who resides a few towns away but has no idea you exist.

Do whatever you want with that information. Hold it close or reach out to him. Finding out he has another child may make him happy, but maybe you've had enough family in your lifetime and don't want to open yourself up to more hurt and rejection.

I wish life could've been different.

I wish I could've been stronger and given you the love you deserved.

At least you have Austin, a boy who's loved you since he took his first breath. His view of you isn't tainted by Colton's hate.

I hope, in my death, you'll embrace your brother and take him under your wing, doing everything you can to protect him from your father or anyone else who would do him harm.

Do not hold my sins against him.

Don't hate the little boy who looks up to you and adores you. He needs you now as much as you need him.

I'm not looking for your forgiveness.

It's too late for that.

I want you to know you are loved.

You were wanted.

But my fear and weakness stopped me from being the mother you deserved.

I hope you find peace and happiness. I wish I could be there to see you as the man you are today. No doubt, strong and hard.

Open your heart to someone.

Let love in. Find peace.

That's my dream for you, my son.

Find the happiness I could never give you.

Love always,

Your Mother

I fold over the sheet of paper and sit there, processing the words as my fingers drift across the black cursive.

The words are nice to read, but they're too late to bring me any solace.

I tuck the note in my pocket, not wanting Austin to find our mother's words. If he found out about Ashton, I'm pretty sure the news would devastate him.

I step outside, and my gran looks up, studying me. "You takin' Austin home?" she asks again, skipping right over the letter.

"I am," I blurt out, not giving myself a chance to overthink the entire situation.

"Good." She smiles and pats the armrest of the chair next to her. "Now sit with this old lady and talk to me. Tomorrow, it's going to be quiet around here."

I ease back into the chair, resting my coffee mug on my knee. "Why don't you come back with us?"

Although I hate this place, I love my grandmother. I should've come home and visited her over the years, but staying away was easier on me. It was the only way I didn't let the bad creep back into my heart.

Absence doesn't make the heart grow fonder, but it sure has allowed me to pretend like my past never happened.

"Don't be silly." She waves me off. "I love it here. There's nowhere else I'd rather live. But make this old woman a promise."

"Anything."

"Don't stay gone so long this time."

"I was an asshole, Gran."

She nods. "You were, but that's in the past. I don't think I have another ten years left either. Maybe I can see you at Christmas."

"Why don't you come to Florida? The weather's great that time of year. I can show you where I work and live. Show you the life I've built for myself."

She smiles again. "I'd love that."

Austin strolls outside, scratching his bare chest as he stretches. "Did I hear Christmas?" he stutters through a yawn.

"You did. I was just talking to your brother about visiting you both for Christmas this year."

Austin's eyes snap to mine. "Visiting us both?" He raises his eyebrows. "I'm coming with you?"

I nod. "But only if you want to."

He fist-pumps the air, letting out a loud howl.

"Hell yeah! Beaches. Babes. Why wouldn't I want to come with you?"

I don't want to burst his bubble, but I live nowhere near beaches, and the babes... Well, they're pretty much like the chicks in Tennessee. "Don't know," I admit.

He'll learn soon enough that the romanticized version of Florida isn't reality.

He starts to walk back toward the door, moving faster than he did when he strolled out. "I'm going to pack." Before he reaches for the handle, he leans down, planting a kiss on Granny's cheek. "I'll miss you, Gran."

"Mm-hm," she mumbles, smiling up at her grandson. "You seem devastated at the news."

"But you're coming for Christmas, right?" he asks.

She nods at him. "I'll be there with my bikini."

He grimaces. "Let's not get crazy, Gran."

She chuckles, shooing him inside, and then turns her gaze toward me. "You're doing right, Pike. I'm proud of you."

I relax back into the chair again. "I don't know about that, but I figure I can't mess him up more than his parents already did."

"And Ashton?" she asks, finally getting to the letter she gave me.

"He doesn't know about me, and I think it's best it stays that way."

She gives me a slow nod, twisting her lips like she wants to give me her opinion, but she won't. "That's your call."

"I know." I take a deep breath, pushing off the chair, needing to get my ass moving. "I better get my girl up so we can hit the road."

Gran's on her feet, arms around my middle before I can make a move toward the door. "I like your girl, Pike. She's good for you. A little high-maintenance, but sweet as apple pie." Her eyes twinkle as she whispers, "You hold on to that one."

I wrap my arms around her, leaning forward to kiss her forehead. "I have every intention of keeping her, Gran."

"That's my boy. Now, scoot. I have lunch with the ladies from church."

"Gran, what do you want to do about Da—" I stop myself, remembering he's not my father. "What do you want to do about Colton?"

She reaches up, cupping my cheek in her small hand. "Nothing, son. Leave him be. He made his bed. Now, it's time he lies in it."

"You know how he was arrested?"

She shakes her head, dropping her hand from my face.

"He attacked Gigi in her apartment. We live next door to each other. I can't figure out why he did it."

"That's something you'll have to ask him. I stopped trying to figure him out a long time ago."

I'm not sure anyone will ever understand Colton Moore. All I know is he's not worth my time or energy.

He's nothing to me.

8

GIGI

"ARE YOU READY FOR THIS?" Pike asks as we sit in my grandmother's driveway with Austin in the backseat, headphones in his ears.

"You think my dad's going to lose it?" I know the answer, but I ask him anyway.

Of course Joe Gallo's going to go off the rails. It's something he does often, and I still haven't gotten used to it.

Pike gives me a forced smile. "I don't know."

I look over my shoulder at Austin and wince. "I know my dad, and he's not easygoing, ya know? He's going to freak out."

Pike laughs, rubbing his forehead.

I cover my face with my hands and groan. "Maybe we should go."

Pike pulls my hand away from my cheeks. "We

have to face him sometime. We can't hide Austin forever."

"What about me?" Austin asks, scooting forward and sticking his face between us. "Where are we?" He looks through the windshield, taking in my grandparents' house. "Whoa. Someone hit the mother lode."

Pike turns his upper body so he's face-to-face with Austin. "This is her grandparents' house. I expect you to be on your best behavior. You understand?"

Austin gives him a lopsided smile, throwing up his hands. "Chill, bro. I'm not a little kid. I know how to act around old people."

I glance toward the ceiling of the truck, knowing this is one giant mistake. "Oh Lord."

"So help me God, if you embarrass me…" Pike's sounding more like a parent than I ever imagined.

It's cute, even.

Austin cocks his head, scrunching up his face. "You need to relax a little. I'll behave. I can charm the pants off almost anyone." He gives Pike a smirk followed by that damn wink.

I bite my lip and shake my head. "Clusterfuck," I mutter to myself.

Pike squeezes my hand, giving me a small smile. "It'll be fine, darlin'."

Austin takes out his earbuds, winding them around his phone, eyes flickering between the two of us. "What's the problem? You two are tense as shit."

"My father's the problem." I turn to look at Austin. "He's not happy about Pike, and now…"

"I'm the bonus prize no one wanted?" Austin raises an eyebrow, his voice filled with sadness.

I frown, hating for him to feel like he's unwanted. "You're wanted. You're just a giant surprise."

"He'll love me," Austin brags, puffing out his chest like he's the shit, his emotions all over the place. "Everyone loves me."

"Let's get it over with. We can sit here all day and talk about how your dad's going to react, or we can go inside and let the chips fall where they may."

Austin reaches for the handle and climbs down from the truck. "Don't worry. We'll be BFFs before the end of the day," he promises.

I'm out of my seat, following him up the driveway, jumping in front of him before he has a chance to knock. I turn to face him, blocking the door with my body. "Listen, I know this is all new for you, but this is important. This is make it or break it time. You understand?"

Austin turns his baseball cap backward and then pounds on his chest with one fist. "I'm bringing my A game, sis."

I roll my eyes. *This kid*. He reminds me of every cocky jock I was ever around in high school, loving himself and thinking he's God's gift to the entire world.

"Don't worry. He'll behave." Pike gives Austin that don't-be-an-asshole look I've seen my father throw my way more than a few times.

We walk in, Pike and Austin behind me, and I hold my breath, knowing there's going to be a shit-storm of questions hurled in our direction.

I'm not even five feet into the foyer when I catch my father's eye. He's sitting in the living room with a clear line of sight to the front door. He sat there on purpose, waiting for us to walk through so he could give Pike the stink-eye.

Typical.

My dad moves his eyes from my face to Pike, and then they land on Austin. He's out of his seat, stalking toward us, jaw set tight, eyes narrowed.

Oh boy.

"Sweetheart," my mother says, stepping right in my father's path and coming out of nowhere. She's like a ninja. He's plastered against her back, glaring at Pike like he just robbed a bank or some shit.

"Hey, Mom." I grab her quickly, hugging her, and throwing my father's glare right back. "I missed you."

"Who's the young, handsome devil with your handsome devil?" she whispers with a giggle.

I release her and glance over my shoulder. "That's Austin, Pike's brother."

"Oh." Mom's body stiffens before she releases me and goes right to him. "My poor baby," Mom says, holding out her arms to Austin like he's one of her own. "I'm Suzy. Gigi's mom."

Austin looks a little freaked out as my mom grabs him and squeezes tightly. "Ma'am," he squeaks, losing his badass edge pretty quick.

"Are you okay?" she asks him.

My mom worries about everyone, and it's totally adorable when it's not aimed at me.

I turn back around, letting my mom do her thing, and bring my gaze back to my father. His body is stiff, arms straight, hands in tight balls at his sides. Is he pissed off? For sure.

I cross my arms, dropping my shoulder, and cock my head, throwing the vibe right back at him. *Whatcha going to say now, big guy?* I raise an eyebrow, waiting for him to open his mouth, but he just tightens his jaw and swallows whatever angry words are sitting on his tongue.

"After the funeral," I say, reminding him that the two men behind me just lost their mother, "Pike felt it was best to bring Austin home for his last year of high school. Family first, right?" I throw his own words right in his face, but I do it with a hint of a smile.

Suck on that, Dad.

"We're so happy you're here," Mom tells Austin. "Family is the most important thing to us, and you're just in time for Sunday dinner. I hope you're hungry."

"I'm starving." Austin rubs his stomach. "Pike's fridge didn't have much in it that was edible."

"I wasn't expecting company," Pike mumbles as he grabs my hand, ignoring my father's angry presence. "You okay?"

I nod. "You?"

"Great," he replies, but not in a way that's convincing at all.

"What's going on out there?" My grandma's voice comes from the kitchen.

"We have an extra guest," Mom calls out, and within three seconds, my grandma is in the foyer, pushing my father out of the way.

"The more, the merrier." Grandma eyes Austin and then looks at Pike. "I can see the resemblance. They build them cute up there in Tennessee."

"Gram," I groan, covering my face in embarrassment.

She touches my cheek, looking at me with nothing but joy. "Sweetie, I'm old, not dead. Guess who's back?" she says to me, holding on to my shoulder.

"Who?" I glance around, seeing no one out of the ordinary besides Austin.

"Tamara and Lily finally came home for summer break." She pitches her thumb over her shoulder toward the lanai. "They're out by the pool."

My eyes widen, and for the first time in days, I'm freaking excited. I've missed Tamara since she wouldn't leave her shit-in-the-pants boyfriend behind, and Lily… I haven't seen her in what feels like forever.

"Can I talk with you?" My father motions toward my grandfather's study, killing all my joy. "Alone," he adds.

I squeeze Pike's hand, trying to smile. "Give us ten. If I'm not out, send in a search party. One of us might not come out alive."

"I'm sorry." Pike blows out a breath, glancing at my father over my shoulder. "This is all my fault."

"It's not your fault. *Stop*. I'll handle my daddy. Trust me." I brush my lips against his before turning around to face a very angry Joe Gallo. "Let's go, Dad," I demand, walking toward the study without even waiting for him.

"Joseph," my mother warns, trying to come to my aid and throwing out his full name like he's about to be in trouble.

"Giovanna."

Ah. He's busting out my full name. That means shit is serious. "Yes, Dad?" I fold my arms again, throwing him all kinds of shade as he closes the doors to the study.

He blows out a loud breath, scrubbing his face with his hands. "Do you really think being involved with a man who has a criminal family and is now in charge of a kid is something you should be getting into in your life right now?"

"Are you for real right now?" I bite out, dropping a shoulder.

He mimics me and crosses his arms too. "As real as you're gonna get."

"So…" I grit my teeth, staring him down. "Pike's father is an asshole, and his mother's dead. None of which Pike was involved in. The kid out there—" I point toward the foyer "—who's seventeen, by the way, has no parents left. What's Pike supposed to do?" I throw up my hands, exasperated. "Just leave him behind to fend for himself?"

My father glances up toward the ceiling as his jaw ticks. "Of course not. Pike did what any man should do in that situation. My issue isn't with what he does in his life. My issue is the choices you're making in your life."

I laugh, putting my hands on my hips. "How old am I?"

"Twenty-two."

"So, I'm an adult, yeah?"

His eyes flash with anger. He knows where I'm going and that I'm right. Lord, the man hates being wrong. "Of course, but I'll never stop being your father."

"Then you should support me instead of getting pissed when I don't do what you want. You know what you've always told me?"

His shoulders slump. He knows I've stored away

every word he's ever spoken for moments like this. "What?" he growls.

"You told me to be strong and be my own person. To follow my heart and never let anyone lead me astray. You taught me, hammering it into my head, that family is the most important thing in the world. We stick by one another no matter what bad shit happens and never turn our back on someone in need."

He raises his chin. "You sure I said all that?"

I nod. "I could go on if you'd like."

He shakes his head and throws up his hands. "Damn it. I wanted something different for you."

"Different?" I arch an eyebrow, challenging him. "Different from what?"

"I wanted your life to be simple and filled with nothing but happiness."

"News flash, Dad, I am happy."

He rolls his shoulder and moves his neck from side to side, grunting. "But this isn't simple. Let me remind you what hasn't been simple."

I roll my eyes. *Here we go.*

"Pike's been arrested and taken to FBI headquarters to be questioned—"

"For something he didn't do," I interrupt.

He holds out his hand to silence me. "He, along with you, sweetheart, was forced into hiding."

"They weren't looking for me."

Again, he gives me the hand. “Men shot up the compound, and from what I hear, Pike put a bullet in a man’s head.”

I grimace. “He saved our lives,” I tell him, because fuck him and this conversation.

That goddamn palm is back up as he continues talking. “Pike’s mom gets assassinated somewhere in there.”

“Again, not Pike’s fault.”

He bristles. “Then, you come home, and Pike’s father is in your apartment and tries to kill you.”

I blow out a breath, squaring my shoulders. “Pike saved me.”

“If it weren’t for fucking Pike, you wouldn’t have needed saving.”

I flinch because my father rarely swears at me, but he just dropped a doozy. “This isn’t his fault,” I groan.

“And now…” He steps forward, dropping his voice. “You come home from his mother’s funeral with a teenager in tow.”

“Family first, Daddy.”

He crosses his arms again, clearly not amused by my words. “Are you going to be a stepmom at twenty-two, Giovanna?”

I shrug. “Austin doesn’t need a mom. He needs a friend and to know that there are still people who care about him. Maybe—” I glare at him. “Maybe instead of making him feel unwelcome, you should get to know the kid whose mother was just murdered while he was in the room."

My father's body jerks. "He was in the room?"

I nod. "They knocked him out, but when he woke up, he found her body."

My father sucks in air between his teeth. "Damn."

"Uh, yeah."

He rubs the back of his neck, head bent toward the floor. "I can't imagine."

"So, instead of being Mr. Judgy McJudgerson, maybe you should try to find out what happened before you fly off the handle first."

"I feel bad for the kid, but I still don't approve of your relationship with Pike."

I step forward, getting right in my dad's face. "Do you hate that I fell in love with a man who's exactly like you?"

"He's nothing like me," my father snaps.

I throw my head back and laugh. "He's so much like you, I should probably get my head examined. I love Pike for all the same reasons I love you, damn it."

"Just don't do something stupid like run off and get married. You two are still so new. It's already complicated enough with Austin. I don't want you to get your heart broken again, baby."

"Dad, we eloped in Tennessee." It's a lie, but I figure he deserves it now.

"What?" His eyes widen, and all the color drains from his face.

"I'm kidding," I snort, putting him out of his misery when, really, I should let him suffer longer.

The vein down the middle of my dad's forehead bulges. "That's not funny."

"It was to me." I smile. "Pike's a really great guy, Dad. You liked him a lot before the bad shit went down. You even pushed me to be friends with him, remember?" I nudge him with my shoulder.

He mumbles under his breath before he clears his throat. "I was an idiot."

"No. *Now* you're being an idiot," I correct him, resting my hand on his bulky forearm. "Be nice to Pike and Austin. They could really use some friends right about now, Daddy."

"Sweetie." My mom's voice comes from the other side of the door before her knock.

"Yeah, sugar?" Dad moves his gaze toward the door, and I use the moment to relax because this has been freaking exhausting.

Mom opens the door, looking between us. "Come out and spend time with the family. Your mother is asking for Gigi, and she told me to tell you to leave the child alone already."

I smirk, but I quickly sober when my father glances at me. "We're done, Mom," I tell her, shutting down the conversation, whether he likes it or not.

She motions toward the door, excusing me. "Give us a minute alone, Gigi."

I nod, smiling at my dad as I close the door behind me.

You're in so much trouble, Daddy.

Someone's going to get their ass chewed out, and for once, it isn't me.

9

PIKE

"YOU'VE HAD a rough few days. Poor baby," Fran says, kneading my shoulders as she stands behind me. "I'll make you feel better."

The woman is harmless.

Her husband, however, is not.

"Fran, get your hands off that boy," Bear growls, eyes locked on her from across the table, looking like he's about to drag her out of the room. "He doesn't need some old lady pawing at him."

Her fingers push harder, working my stiff shoulders like a pro. "You love when I do this for you," she tells him, earning herself a slow headshake from Bear.

He cocks an eyebrow, and his jaw tenses. "He has his own woman to do that."

Gigi stalks into the kitchen, shaking her head as

soon as she sees Fran's hands on me. "Aunt Fran, you just can't keep your hands to yourself, can you?"

"You takin' over?" Fran asks Gigi.

Gigi glances down at me and winks but looks up at Fran a moment later. "I was going to see Lily and Tamara, but if your hands are tired, I will."

Well, there went my rescue.

"I'm good, doll. I can do this all day."

I can just imagine the shit-eating smirk on Fran's face as she said those words. And based on the scowl on Bear's face, I'm not far off.

"I could use some air." I pat Fran's hand on my shoulder as I push back from the table, finding a way out.

"I'll be waiting if you need another rubdown." Fran winks at me, and my face instantly heats.

"Like hell you will, woman. Get over here and give me those lips." Bear taps his leg, and Fran moves around the table, doing as she's told. "Good girl," he says, rewarding her with a deep kiss as soon as she's firmly planted in his lap.

"How'd it go?" I ask Gigi, pulling her off to the side before she can sneak out to the patio with her cousins.

"Fine." She rolls her eyes. "You know how he is, but I think we made headway."

"You made headway, or he did?"

"We did." She shrugs and snickers. "Well, I did."

I look over her shoulder, watching as her father stalks through the living room, clearly not happy. "Maybe I should talk to him."

She slides her hand up my chest, resting her palm on my shoulder, drawing my attention back to her. "Don't do that. I really took care of everything."

I'm sure she thinks she did, but I need to have another man-to-man talk with her father. This shit needs to end. "Thanks, darlin'," I tell her, brushing my lips lightly against hers.

"Where's Austin?" she asks, all sugary-sweet and totally trying to change the subject.

I shift my gaze toward the pool, catching sight of the Casanova lying between the two girls. "He's outside with your cousins."

"Shoot," she grumbles and shakes her head. "He better not get any ideas."

I laugh. "He's seventeen. All he has are ideas."

She chuckles, pushing me away before dashing out the door.

"Gigi!" The two women run toward her, almost knocking her off her feet as they hug.

Austin's eyes find mine, and I mouth *behave* before sliding the door closed again, leaving them be.

"Pike, can we talk?" James asks.

I nearly jump out of my skin because the man just

appeared out of nowhere. "What's up?" I try to sound casual, like he didn't just scare the living shit out of me.

He motions toward the dining room and waits for me to make the first move, lifting an eyebrow like he's talking in code. "I have some news," he blurts out.

James always has news. The man never stops digging, and with all his contacts in the legal and criminal worlds, I'm sure he always has something crossing his desk.

"Thomas, you comin'?" James yells across the room to where Thomas is watching the Cubs game with the other guys.

I barely have my ass in the dining chair before James starts to speak. "Your father was arraigned two days ago. No bail, so he's going to be behind bars until his trial."

I place my palms on top of the table, trying to be relaxed, but happy as freaking fuck. "More than one charge, I hope?"

James nods. "So many, but the biggest are money laundering, conspiracy, attempted murder, and murder."

I raise my eyebrows. "Murder?"

"He killed a man back in Tennessee before stealing his car and heading here," James replies before blowing out a long breath.

"He's a heartless SOB," I mutter, but this is Colton Moore, and he's always been cold-blooded.

"That he is," Thomas agrees, resting his hand on my shoulder like I need comfort.

"We haven't been able to find out why he was in Gigi's apartment or why he came to Florida. We're sure it has something to do with you, but we haven't pieced it together yet."

"Maybe he wanted to kill me too." I shrug. Anything's possible, especially when it comes to him.

Thomas takes a step back, crossing his arms as he studies me. "Maybe he thought he was in your apartment."

"It's possible." I nod.

James pulls out the chair at the head of the table and sits. "I got word from Tiny and Morris. They're headed this way for business."

"Okay," I draw out, leaning forward and thinking there has to be something more to the story because there always is.

James glances at Thomas briefly before he explains, "They'll want to see you. They know you were at your mother's funeral. They held off on coming to this coast until they knew you'd be back. Should be here in a few days."

I nod, always happy to see the guys, especially since they saved our asses without asking for anything in return. "I'm sure Morris will reach out."

James rests his hands on the table and pushes back, straightening his shoulders. "They're going to ask for payback," he tells me, like his words aren't a big fucking deal.

And they are…they're a *huge* fucking deal.

"Payback for what?" I ask, looking between James and Thomas.

"They lost a lot in that gunfight with DiSantis's men. They're going to want something for that."

I squeeze my hands together, not liking the sound of this. How could they willingly come to my rescue, pretending to be my friend, and then ask for something in return? "What's their price?"

James throws up his hands as he shrugs, not looking rattled in the least. "Fuck if I know, but I'm sure it's going to be big."

"I don't have jack to my name," I admit, and I don't. I have enough to live, but by no means do I have a pile of money sitting in the bank for moments like this.

Thomas laughs, shaking his head at me like I'm an idiot. "They don't want money. They'll want a favor. When they ask, if they ask you and not us, talk to us before you give them an answer. Got it?"

I cross my arms over my chest, trying not to take offense. "Didn't know I had to run my life decisions by you two."

I know I'm an idiot. I shouldn't be smarting off to

the two guys who have saved my ass more times than anyone else ever has in my life.

"Pike." Thomas leans over the table, crowding my space. "You lived with these guys. You know how they operate. You want a cell right next to your pops?"

I shake my head, gritting my teeth. "No," I growl, keeping my eyes on James and not the scary-as-fuck guy looming over me.

"Then talk to us before you make a move," Thomas whispers so quietly, the hairs on my arm stand up like even they want to get away from him.

"What's wrong?" Izzy's in the doorway to the dining room, gaze sweeping between the three of us. "You three together never means good things."

"What's happening?" Joe questions, coming to stand behind her, eyes flickering around the room just like his sister.

Fucking great. I rub my temples, wishing this family weren't so far up one another's asses all the time. Don't get me wrong. It's nice…sometimes. But other times, moments like this, it's all just too much.

James slides out of his chair and moves toward his wife, trying to usher her out of the room. "Nothing's going on. Just having a chat with the kid."

Joe stalks in and sits in the chair James just vacated. "Can I talk to Pike alone?" His ice-cold eyes never leave mine.

"You two going to be okay in here?" Izzy asks,

always looking out for everyone. She's such a ball-buster, but the woman has a good heart.

"We'll be fine," Joe answers for us both, waiting for them to leave, eyes still burning with anger.

"I'm sorry," I blurt as soon as we're alone. "I shouldn't have brought Austin here."

Joe slowly rubs his hands together, grinding his teeth like he's almost choking on whatever he's about to tell me. "I talked to Gigi, and she really laid into me about how I feel about you and how I talk to you."

I raise both my eyebrows, but I don't move another muscle. "Yeah?"

"Yeah." He moves his hand to his face as he passes his fingertips across the stubble of his jaw. "It wasn't pretty, but she reminded me of a few things. Listen…" He pauses, swallowing down what I assume is his pride. "Ever since I found out about you being with my daughter, I haven't been nice to you. I have to keep reminding myself that she's not a little girl anymore."

I give him a halfhearted smile. "She reminds me of that every day."

It's his turn to raise his eyebrows.

"I mean, she keeps telling me she can do whatever she wants. She sure as hell doesn't listen to me," I add.

"I taught her to be strong and independent. I also taught her about loyalty and love."

"Your daughter is truly the most spectacular woman I've ever met, Joe. She's everything," I admit.

"I'm going to back off, but if you fuck up—" he points at me "—don't think I won't kick your ass," he threatens, scratching at his face like he's having an allergic reaction to the entire conversation.

"You can try," I tease, winking at him, hoping to get back to the easy relationship we had when I first started at Inked.

He doesn't even crack a smile. "Now, about your brother."

Here we go.

"We could use some help at Inked. We need someone to run the front desk. I realize he can't work late once school starts, but maybe he can work a few hours in the evenings and on the weekends."

All I can do is blink.

"You'll be able to keep an eye on him, and he'll get to know the rest of us."

Who is this man? I don't know what Gigi said to him in their little chat, but whatever it was, it must've been a freaking killer.

I blink again, waiting for him to say he's totally fucking with me. "You really want him to work at Inked? I mean, he may be a total shit human being."

His eyes don't even twitch as he asks, "He's your brother, yeah?"

I nod slowly because he is, but… "He's my family,

and now that our parents can't raise him, he's fallen on to me and is my responsibility. But I barely know the kid, Joe. Like I said, he could be a total fuckup."

"Are you serious, bro?" Austin thunders, standing just a few feet away, listening to our private conversation. "I'm just a responsibility?"

Fuck. I rush from my seat, trying to get to him, but he's already on the move.

"You know what, fuck you!" he shouts, and everyone in the room flinches. He waves his hand around the room toward Gigi's family. "And fuck them!"

The wide-eyed looks from every Gallo make my stomach turn. They've been nothing but kind and don't deserve this shit.

"Austin, watch your mouth," I grit out, trying to get my hands on him, but he's too damn fast.

The little shit dodges to the right, stalking toward the front door. "I'm out of here. I don't want to be a burden to anyone, especially my own flesh and blood," he rages before storming out the front door, slamming it so damn hard, the photos on the walls rattle.

Before I can chase after him, a hand is on my shoulder, stopping me. "I'll go talk to him," Tamara offers, looking up at me with a sad smile. "He needs some time to cool off. That's all. It'll be okay."

I nod, knowing he's not going to listen to me right

now. If I were in his shoes, I wouldn't listen to me either. I fucked up. I didn't mean for my words to come out that way, and I sure as fuck didn't expect for him to hear them.

"I'm so sorry," I say, looking around the room at the people who've been nothing but nice, making me feel welcome.

Gigi's at my side, wrapping her arm around me and placing a hand on my chest. "It's all going to be okay," she says softly and so damn sweetly.

"Pike." Joe motions for me to come back to the scene of the emotional crime, but there's a different look in his eyes. It's not murder or hate, but...understanding and sadness?

I move toward him, but Gigi stays with me, watching her father, assuming he's going to pull the asshole card.

Joe rubs the back of his neck, eyeballing his daughter before glancing at me. "I've dealt with a lot of teenagers in my life. Sure as hell dealt with emotional ones too. Have three girls, and you'll know the sheer and utter chaos they create." He gives me a smile. "Your brother's going through some shit. Your words hurt him. Let him cool off and he'll come back, but you need to make sure he knows exactly how you feel. Don't hold back, and don't give him enough rope to hang himself either. Be firm yet kind. What happened here can never happen again."

I nod, feeling the knot in my stomach grow tighter. "I know. I'm sorry."

"Don't apologize for him. You did nothing wrong, son."

Son. I blink. Did Joe Gallo just call me son? No one, and I mean no one, has ever called me that. Not even Colton Moore. It was always some mix of bastard and fucker with a few other slurs thrown in to remind me what an insignificant piece of shit I really was. But here, in this moment, with this man who isn't my biggest fan…he called me son.

I swallow, somehow finding my words. "How long do I give him?" I croak, trying to keep the emotion from my voice. Because…*it's just a word, dumbass.*

"Let him come to you." Joe ticks his head toward the dining room where we'd just been sitting.

"Let's eat, have a drink, and wait him out. Tamara will bring him back."

"What if he doesn't come back?"

Joe laughs, slapping me on the shoulder. "Where the hell's he going to go? We're in the middle of nowhere with nothing for miles except bugs and trees."

Gigi tugs at my hand, drawing my attention away from her father as he walks away, leaving us alone. "What set him off? He was just outside flirting with the girls, and then that." She waves her hand toward the door, wrinkling her nose.

I glance down at my feet and shake my head. "I fucked up."

"I can see that." She moves in front of me, touching my face with her fingertips, making me look at her. "But how?"

"I said dumb shit like I always do, but this time, he heard me."

She grimaces. "Stop being so hard on yourself. We all mess up sometimes. I'm sure once he calms down, you'll be able to explain."

I close my eyes, leaning my head forward until our foreheads touch. "Your family has to hate him."

Gigi snorts and pulls away from me so I can see her. "Please, temper tantrums are nothing new around here. He may have used a little bit more colorful language than usual, but it'll be just a distant memory in a few weeks."

I force a smile on to my face, but it's totally fake. "Yeah. Maybe."

"Hey." She bumps my shoulder, probably feeling my *I don't believe a word you're saying* vibe. "My family knows he just lost his mom and his father too. That has to be weighing pretty heavy on him. I'm sure I'd be a complete asshole if I were in his shoes."

I shake my head, drawing in the longest, deepest breath, trying to calm myself. "You're right," I tell her, which gets me an eyebrow raise.

"Can you say that again?" she asks, a crooked smile crossing her face.

"Why?"

She pulls her phone from her back pocket, shaking it in my face. "I want to get that for posterity."

Fuck me. This chick.

10

GIGI

"I'm going to choke him." Pike runs his fingers through his hair as he hunches over his legs while we sit on the couch in his living room. "I swear to God…"

"Stop." I rub his back, rolling my eyes. "They're on their way back. It's not *that* big of a deal."

Austin wasn't the first person to throw a fit and storm out of my grandparents' house. Lord knows he isn't going to be the last. There isn't a person in my family who isn't overdramatic, and Austin seemed to fit right in within the first hour.

Pike lifts his head, eyes blazing. "Not that big of a deal?"

I push his face back toward the floor. "He's a teenager. They do this stuff all the time. I'm sure you did too."

Pike grunts, his back muscles tensing under my fingertips. "Not if you didn't want to get your ass beat."

The frown on my lips is immediate. "Promise me you're not going to hit him."

His eyes are back on me, neck craned, those beautiful brown eyebrows drawn inward. "Do you seriously think I'd hit him?"

My shrug is barely there, but Pike catches it. I grimace and try to make up for it by saying, "Never."

Pike straightens as my hand falls down to the couch near his ass. "Listen, darlin', and listen good."

I nod when he pauses, straightening my back too because I know this is going to be a short but deep conversation.

"I have never put my hands on anyone in my family. I will never put my hands on my brother." He squeezes my hands in his. "Even if the little fucker hits me first, I'll never lay a hand on him."

"I believe you," I confess because I've never seen Pike be physically menacing to anyone unless he hated them and they totally deserved the anger.

"I'd never touch you either. You could stab me in the thigh with a butter knife." I wince because who the fuck would do that, but he just keeps on talking. "There isn't anything you could do to make me hurt you."

"I know." The man would and almost did take a

bullet for me. He's never, even when I've been a complete asshole, shown any type of anger or hostility toward me that's caused me to so much as flinch. He's always sweet in that Pike kind of way.

A few of his fingers brush the hair away from my cheek as his eyes search mine. "I need you to know what I'm saying is true. Never. Never. Never would I lay a hand on you. I'm not built that way."

"I know," I repeat, and I'm being one-hundred-percent truthful, but the look in his eyes tells me he's not believing a single word.

"No. You need to believe what I'm saying. I saw too much bad shit in my life." He shakes his head, pain all over his face. "I'd never want that type of shit to touch you. There's nothing worse than a person you love laying their hands on you in anger, making you not only feel the pain of the strike, but the bite of their words."

My stomach clenches. "Pike," I whisper, moving my cheek into his touch. "I know with everything I am, you'll never hurt me. I promise." I place my hand over his. "I can't imagine what you went through as a kid, and I never want you to feel that way again."

"In ten years, I've never allowed anyone close enough to me to give me that kind of hurt." His eyes sweep across my face as he traces the edge of my chin with his thumb. "Only you, Gigi."

"Only me?" My mouth hangs open. *Only me.*

That's a pretty damn big deal. Pike isn't the first man I've let get close to me. I have two assholes in my past and the scars from the horrific end to those relationships to prove it too.

He nods ever so slightly. "I never wanted to give anyone that power over me. I swore I'd never let anyone else in, but you…" His voice trails off.

I lock on to those green eyes that first captured my attention. "I'm glad you let me in," I whisper.

The door creaks open, and neither of us moves. "Stay calm," I mouth to him with my back to the door, seeing the vein in his neck start to pulse.

A second later, Pike swings his gaze to the front door, and his fingers tighten near my neck. Two distinct sets of footsteps stomp on the tile, followed by two different giggles.

"Hey, bro," Austin barks before laughing again. "Sup?"

"Aussie, what'd I tell you about how to talk to him?" Tamara chastises him, slurring her words a bit.

I close my eyes and count to five, knowing when I turn around, I'm not going to like what I see.

How do I know? Pike's about as hard as a piece of granite and barely breathing.

"I love when you call me that," Austin tells Tamara before there's a loud *umph* and my body dips from the weight.

Pike follows the movement with his eyes, looking

over my shoulder like every promise and word he just said is about to go right out the window.

Uh oh.

"You can sit here, TamTam," Austin offers playfully, and I hear the sound of his hand slapping something.

"Do *not* sit on his lap," Pike growls, his eyes narrowing but not moving from his brother.

"When did Mr. Badass Biker dude turn into such a party pooper?" Tamara teases, her shadow covering me as she stands somewhere behind my back.

"Calm down, big guy." Austin snorts. "We're just having fun, and Tam's my new BFF."

I close my eyes again, trying not to lose my shit because if we both do…it's game over.

"Actually, she's my only friend."

"When school starts, all the girls are going to be all over you, Aussie. You're going to have to fight them off," Tamara tells him.

I let out a sigh, turning to find my cousin leaning her hip against the couch just above Austin as he kicks back, one ankle resting on the knee of his other leg. "A guy can dream, TamTam," he mutters.

What. The. Fuck?

Five hours ago, these two didn't even know each other. Now…now, they have cute nicknames for each other?

TamTam and Aussie.

Puke.

My gaze travels up Tamara's body and lands on her flushed cheeks from too much sun and… "Have you been drinking?"

Tamara shrugs, unable to hide her lopsided smile. "We may have grabbed a few twenty-fours."

My eyes widen, darting from Tamara to Austin. "What the hell? You're both underage."

Tamara taps her purse slung over her shoulder. "I still have my ID from Daytona." She winks.

I glance toward the ceiling and mutter, "Dear God," before sucking in a breath. I'm going to lose my shit. "He's in high school, Tam. High school!" I glare at her.

She wrinkles her nose, leering at me. "Hey, Ms. Prude. I know you had a hell of a lot more than a twenty-four or two when you were his age—or mine, for that matter." She throws her chin at Pike, and I know she's talking about *that night.* "Hypocrite much?"

Oh. My. God.

I suddenly sounded like my father or mother. Take your pick. They were both the same when it came to underage drinking and partying. But now the words are coming out of my mouth about a kid who isn't even my own. I shake my head, trying to remember I'm not the mom of these two assholes. "I'm not a hypocrite."

"You so are," she argues with a smug grin as she

rests her bent arm on Austin's shoulder. "Never thought I'd see the day you'd turn into Suzy."

Pike's hand is on my leg, squeezing tight enough to draw my attention away from the giggling idiots. "Let it go," he says softly. "Just let it go."

Tamara moves, wedging herself between my back and Austin's side. "What are we going to do tonight?" she asks like nothing happened earlier and it's just another day.

"We're going home," I tell her, leering over my shoulder at her.

Her eyes widen, and she jerks her head back. "The party's just getting started, li'l cuz. What's at home besides *nothing?*"

She has a point. I still hadn't had time to buy any furniture. Hell, there isn't even a spoon or a coffee cup in the kitchen. Everything is in my parents' garage, waiting to be picked up. Well, not everything. I still have to buy things. So many things too. But who has time to shop when death and mayhem are falling all around? Not this girl.

"Fine, I'm taking you to your parents', then," I demand, pushing her away from me when I try to stand.

But I don't make it to my feet before Pike's hand is around my wrist, pulling me back onto the couch. "Stay here tonight."

I blink. "Here?" I repeat.

"Please," he begs.

"I have Tam to consider."

"So? I have Austin."

"Sleepover!" Tamara shouts, fist-pumping the air.

Austin nods with a smug grin I wish I could wipe right off his face. "Nothing sounds better."

Sweet Jesus. Nothing about this sounds like a good idea. "I don't think…" I mutter.

"I'll feel safer if you're here," Pike says, cutting me off as I snap my lips shut because I feel safer here too.

"Pike," I breathe.

"I need you here tonight," Pike admits, his eyes pleading with me to say yes.

"Ew," Tamara gags. "I don't want to listen to you two bumping uglies all night."

I shoot my cousin a death look. "You better shut it before I shut it for you."

She sticks out her tongue, proving we're never too old to act like immature kids. "Whatever," she mutters, snuggling a little too close to Austin.

"You like wearing orange?" I snap at her.

She wrinkles that cute-ass nose on her beautiful face. "I hate it, but it looks great with my complexion."

There isn't a color that looks bad on her with her deep olive skin, a perfect mix of her Italian father and African American mother. She looks perpetually suntanned, while I, thanks to my fair-skinned blond mother, don't.

"If you keep touching him, you're going to wind up behind bars since he's seventeen."

Austin throws his arm around Tamara. "Nah, babe. I checked the laws. We're good."

Tamara's gaze slowly slides to Austin. "It's never happening, kid."

Austin shrugs. "I can wait a year."

Tamara smacks his chest, giggling again because she's drunk and an idiot. "You're such an asshole."

"Stay here so I don't murder him," Pike whispers, his mouth right next to my ear.

I giggle, sounding just like my moronic cousin, and turn my head so our lips are almost touching. "Don't worry. She likes her men a bit older, baby." I waggle my eyebrows because by older, I mean *older.* "She's just being a pain in the ass."

"Tamara can take the spare." Pike frowns, catching himself because we all know it's not spare anymore. "I mean Austin's room, and Austin can sleep on the couch."

"And Gigi?" Austin asks, raising an eyebrow, chin lifted, just trying to give Pike a hard time.

"I'll sleep with Tam," I say quickly, ending whatever game Austin is trying to play.

Pike grunts. "Fucker."

"Ooh. Let's make popcorn and watch a romantic

comedy, yeah?" Tam asks, popping up from the couch and clapping her hands. "Like old times, Gig." She bumps my shoulder with her hip, knowing I'm an absolute sucker for anything romance.

"I get my own bowl," Austin announces, lifting his shirt with his fingertips and scratching at his six-pack. "I don't share."

"Shocking." Tamara winks at him.

"What can I say?" he asks, lifting his shirt even more, flashing the entire room. "I'm greedy."

I roll my eyes.

"Everyone can have their own bowl," Pike says easily, like he's not so freaking tense he could shatter. "Guys on the floor, girls on the couch."

Austin looks cross-eyed at Pike.

"I don't want any hands wandering," Pike grumbles.

Tamara leans forward, bending at the waist, and loses her shit in a fit of laughter. "Listen..." She slaps her knee, snorting. "Austin is cute and all."

"Cute?" His eyes widen like he's truly offended. "I'm hot, TamTam."

"Whatever," she teases, waving him off, "but I like my guys with a little more..." She pauses, eyes sweeping over him and the six-pack he's still showing. "Hair on their chest."

"Baby," Austin quips, that smug grin right back on his lips. "I got all the hair you could ever need."

I snicker at the insanity of the entire situation, and I figure it's best I just throw her business out there so there's no room for misinterpretation. "She likes 'em *old*, Austin. Real old."

Tamara rears her leg back and kicks the side of my calf. "Don't be an asshole. Pike isn't a youngster."

I rub the spot that will no doubt bruise from her bony-ass toes. "Pike's *only* five years older than me. How old was that one guy?" I ask her, forgetting his name because he wasn't around long enough for me to even memorize it.

"Marcus?" she asks, tapping her chin with her index finger.

"No. I remember Marcus. That other one. The one with the gray hair."

Austin's face pales, and he looks like he's going to puke. "Tam. Why you hittin' the old shit?"

She smacks him right upside the head without giving two shits if it hurts him or not. "Shut your hole, li'l boy. And his name was George."

I snort. "George."

"Yup." Austin slowly shakes his head, touching the spot where she just smacked him. "George sounds like an old-ass fucker." He moves, flinching as she reaches back, ready to hit him again. "Don't do it, woman," he warns her, but there's a playful smirk on his face. "You'll be sorry, old-man fucker."

"Dear God," Pike mutters at my side, and when I

turn to face him, he has his eyes closed, nostrils flaring like he's just smelled the biggest pile of shit.

"Can we just watch the damn movie?" Tamara asks, crossing her arms and dropping one shoulder, clearly not liking us talking about her choice in men.

"Your dad know about the old guys?" Austin asks, not reading her body language at all.

"Nope, and if he finds out—" she bends down, getting right in his face "—you better sleep with one eye open, Aussie." She ruffles his hair when the look of horror flashes on his face. "Now." She clears her throat and straightens, putting on a big smile. "Where's the popcorn?"

This is going to be a long-ass night.

11

PIKE

"THE KIDS ARE STILL ASLEEP," I whisper in Gigi's ear as I cage her in with my arms.

She leans forward, resting her hip against the kitchen counter, her fingers wrapped around the coffee mug as she gawks at me. "Kids?"

I nod. "Yep. Tam and Austin are out cold. I'm sure we have a little time before they wake up."

"Time for what?" She lifts an eyebrow.

I waggle mine, sliding my hand to her hip and squeezing. "You know."

She glances at Austin on the couch, his mouth hanging open with his arm slung over his face. "We can't. What if they hear?"

"Fine, at least take a shower with me," I plead, knowing once I have her naked, all bets are off.

She eyes me for a moment, studying my face, but

I'm not giving in. "Well, I do need a shower, but Tam and I are going shopping soon."

I grab the coffee from her hands, setting the cup on the counter. "She's dead nuts asleep. You aren't leaving anytime soon, and I know how to be quick."

"You better behave," she tells me, poking me in the chest.

I smirk. "When don't I behave?"

She rolls her eyes. "Always."

In one quick motion, I find the elastic at her waistband, dipping my fingers inside enough to find the patch of skin that always drives her wild. "Scout's honor."

I tug her down the hallway toward the bedroom before she has a chance to protest. She pauses just outside Tamara's doorway, glancing around the corner to make sure she's still sleeping.

Tugging her arm again, I pull her toward my bedroom. "Stop wasting time, darlin'."

I push the door closed with my ass and hook my fingers into the top of my sweat pants, quickly removing them.

She shakes her head, giggling a little bit and blushing like she hasn't seen my cock before. "We *seriously* can't do this."

I pitch my thumb toward the door, my pants down around my ankles and my cock standing at full attention as I move us into the adjoining bathroom. "They won't hear a thing. Turn on the water."

She reaches over me, doing exactly what I ask. Before she has time to make another excuse, my hands are at her sides, lifting her tank top over her head, exposing her beautiful breasts. "God, I've missed these."

She cups her breasts, taunting me as she runs her thumbs over her hardened nipples. "You make it sound like you haven't seen them in ages."

My cock bobs, doing its own thing, as happy as the rest of me to see my girl naked again. "It feels like forever. Last time, it was dark."

She reaches down, her eyes on me, and pulls down her shorts, kicking them off to the side. "Lock the door. I don't need them walking in on anything."

I reach back, not taking my eyes off her as I engage the lock, making sure no one can walk in on us. "They have their own bathroom."

She gives me a look. One I can't really place, but I know something I said is wrong. "They better not be fucking in their bathroom too."

"God. No," I tell her, because I'd had that talk with Austin last night once his dumb ass finally sobered up. He wasn't laying a finger or cock on Tamara Gallo or any Gallo, for that matter. Ever. "That's not what I meant. Now give me your mouth. You're wasting time."

She steps back into the warm spray, motioning for me to follow her. I don't hesitate as I step into the tiny shower, the hot water streaming over my skin as I wrap my arms around her waist and pull her body to me.

"I've been waiting for this," I murmur against her lips, having missed her mouth. Her warmth. Her touch.

She pulls away, kneeling down as her hand wraps around my cock, stroking it. "I've been waiting for this." She licks her lips, inching toward my cock as it takes everything in me not to grab her head and shove my dick right into her mouth.

Her lips close around the head of my cock, and I thrust my hips forward, begging for more. She moans, her hand working up and down the shaft, and I close my eyes to stop myself from coming. Seeing her kneeling before me, sucking my dick, is more than I can take. The last thing I want is to be a two-pump chump, coming in her mouth before she's barely had a chance to get started.

The heat of her mouth mixes with the warm spray of the shower, setting my entire body on fire. I comb my fingers through her hair, touching her head gently as I rock my hips forward, wanting her to suck me deeper.

She hums her enjoyment, probably getting off on the fact that my legs are almost shaking. With one hand on the wall, I try to steady myself, locking every muscle in my body to stay upright.

"Am I doing this okay?" she asks, stopping her sweet sucking and causing me to open my eyes.

"Perfect, darlin'. Just fucking perfect."

She smiles up at me, stroking my cock with one hand and placing her other hand between her legs.

Sweet Jesus. I can't wait. I can't. But goddamn do I want to. I drop my head, back pressed against the wall, watching her fingers play with her pussy as her lips close back around me.

If this isn't heaven, I don't ever want to go. The beautiful creature before me, all sweet and good, has a dirty streak that makes my dick hard without even trying. But having her on her knees, water cascading over her breasts, fingering her pussy, is nothing short of the most perfect moment of my life.

"Stop," I moan, barely able to take it anymore. "I can't..."

She looks up, my cock between her lips, eyes wide. "What's wrong?" she asks, but it's barely audible as she speaks around my dick.

My hands are under her arms, hauling her upward until she locks her legs around my waist. "It was too much. Too perfect," I tell her when her eyes flash with worry. "You said you'd behave, and you lied."

She smirks, biting her lip.

Reaching between us, I grab my cock, lining it up perfectly with her greedy, beautiful cunt. "No moaning." I motion toward the bedroom with my head, reminding her we're not alone.

"Kiss me, then," she breathes.

I take her mouth with mine, sliding my cock into her slowly, taking what's mine.

12

GIGI

"WELL, SOMEONE LOOKS SATISFIED," Tamara teases over the brim of her coffee mug, sitting at Pike's kitchen table and quirking an eyebrow.

"Shut up." I wave her off, feeling the heat creep up my neck and settling on my face.

Her eyes never leave me as she sips her coffee and tilts her head. "I'm really impressed. I thought you'd be a loud one for sure."

My fingers bunch around the dish towel on the counter before I hurl it in her direction, catching her off guard. It slaps her in the face but luckily misses her coffee. "Nice," she taunts, tossing the cloth onto the table in front of her. "You're so fucking chatty sometimes, I figured when you were getting it, you'd be all *oh yes* or *harder*."

I narrow my eyes on her because the way she said

those words was pretty fucking loud and sexy as hell too. "I never sound like that." I stick out my tongue, going back to the cup of coffee I started an hour ago.

Her finger taps against the mug as she studies me, but I do my best not to look at her. "So, you're the silent type?"

I roll my eyes as I reach for the coffeepot, topping off what's left in my mug. "You don't need to know how I am in the…you know."

Tamara laughs, shaking her head at me. "You're so lame. Beyond lame."

Leaning forward, I wrap my fingers around the mug, gawking at my smartass cousin. "Do you screech like a howler monkey?"

She smirks. "Since we're going to be roomies, you just may find out."

I hold in the gag that's building in the back of my throat. "What happened to your guy?"

She shrugs, twisting her lips. "I kicked his ass to the curb. I was done playing with boys, and it's time I find myself a real man again."

"A real man?" I lift an eyebrow, looking at her in her pink bunny pajamas as she talks about the difference between men and boys. "Cute pjs."

"Shut your mouth." She glares at me before barking out a laugh. "They're comfy, and I didn't have time to get all the shit out of my car. They were the first thing I found." She leans forward, resting her elbows on the table and lets out a loud sigh.

"So, what really happened to him?" I'm talking about her boyfriend, and she knows it.

"He was getting a little too territorial, and I'd had enough. Sometimes, it's cute, but then other times…" She looks up at me with her hazel eyes blazing. "I knew when I wanted to suffocate him in his sleep, it was time to go."

I nod, knowing once murder comes into play, it's time to pull up stakes and move on. "You finally came to your senses."

"And you know what they say?"

I shrug, because she could be going anywhere with this statement. Anywhere.

"Tattooed boys are my favorite toys." She smirks.

I roll my eyes again. "You're such a weirdo."

"Pike has tats," she reminds me like I've forgotten.

"And?" I snort.

"He's a great toy, isn't he? Better than what's his name?" She taps her chin like my list of guys is so damn long she can't remember.

Bullshitter.

"Erik," I croak, even though she hasn't forgotten.

"And that dipshit Keith. Neither were real men. But Pike…" Her gaze shifts to behind me, and I know he's there. I feel his body heat and presence before he can say a word. "…is all man."

Pike grunts, pulling the cup of coffee from my hand and lifting it to his lips. Before I can warn him, he takes a large gulp and immediately winces. "Jesus, darlin'. This tastes like shit."

I reach out to take the mug from him, but he dumps the contents into the sink before I can rescue my cold coffee. "I was enjoying that," I whine.

"It was cold and the amount of sugar in it..."

"I like my coffee sweet." I snarl because I needed caffeine, and twice now, he's denied me. First with sex, not that I'm complaining, and now, by throwing it out like it wasn't any good, which it was.

He doesn't speak as he turns his back to Tamara and me, busying himself with making us a new pot of coffee.

"He's so hot," Tamara mouths, totally checking out his ass. Her eyes are hungry as they travel upward, taking in the bare skin of his back, which does, in fact, have ink too. "So freaking hot." She hoists two thumbs in the air, lifting her eyebrows with the biggest damn smile.

"What's on tap today?" Pike asks, turning around just as Tamara's putting her hands down, and he's completely oblivious to the fact that she was just treating him like a piece of meat.

"We're going shopping," I tell Pike, leaning against him as the coffee starts to brew behind us. "If I can ever finish a cup of coffee."

His hand is on my waist, squeezing ever so gently. "I'll take you guys."

"No," Tamara declares, shaking her head quickly. "I want a girls' day. We have so much to catch up on."

Pike glances down at me, and I shrug because nothing had been set in stone. "So, you two are going to talk about me?" he asks with a tiny smirk.

"Pretty much," Tamara answers, rising from the table to come stand at the other side of the countertop. "And it's going to be pretty damn hard to get all the juicy bits if you're there."

"There're no juicy bits," I lie because, holy freaking hell, there's so much to tell her.

Her eyes rake over him again, but now she's checking out his chest, the tats, all the way down to his happy trail. "Girl, if you don't have a juicy bit to share, then you're clearly doing something wrong."

She is such a ho. "Go get dressed before you embarrass yourself."

"Mornin'," Austin drawls as he saunters into the kitchen, his eyes little slits as he scratches at his stomach like he has a rash. "What time is it?" He blinks slowly as he takes in Tamara in her super-short shorts and bunny tank top that hugs every curve and nipple the girl has.

"Noon," she answers, eyes moving to him for only a second before coming back to my guy. "They've been up for a while."

My hand is around whatever's in front of me, sending it flying through the air and, again, hitting her straight in the face. She pulls the oven mitt away, tossing it back, but I catch it. "Why don't you go get dressed, Tam?"

Austin's just standing there, watching us, eyes wide and totally zeroed in on her hard nipples. "Don't get dressed on my account," he teases with a grin.

I'm pretty sure if I looked close enough at his face, he'd be drooling.

Pike slides a new cup of coffee in front of me, the steam rising above my face. "Austin and I have some shit to do today too."

Austin's eyes finally leave Tamara's tits and look at his brother as he plops onto a stool near the counter. "Like what?"

"Got to get you a new ID, and Joe said something about hiring you on at Inked if you're interested in a job."

"No shit," Austin whispers in disbelief.

"My dad said that?" I gape at Pike, blinking rapidly. "You sure you heard him right?"

Pike nods, those green eyes sweeping across my face. "Those were his exact words."

"Before all the fucks or after?" Tamara asks, reminding us all about the meltdown.

I give her the side-eye, and she shrugs.

"Fuck," Austin mutters, dropping his shoulders,

remorse clearly evident in his posture. "I'm so fucking sorry. So. So. So. Fucking sorry."

"Maybe try talking without so many fucks, kid." Tamara chuckles. "I mean, we all love the word, but I'm thinking at the shop, it may not fly around so freely."

I snort. "We're not a library," I remind her. It is a business, of course, but it's still a tattoo shop. "But you should probably expand your vocabulary if my dad hires you."

"I fu…screwed up, didn't I?" Austin's eyes are begging me to tell him he didn't, but I have to be honest.

"Kinda. But…" I give him a small smile, hoping I can at least make him feel a little better. "We've all screwed up before. It's not the end of the world."

"Go shower, and we'll head to the shop and see how bad the damage is," Pike tells him, getting a quick nod from Austin before he takes off back down the hallway.

"You're really sure you heard my dad say he wanted to hire him?" I scrunch my nose. "Because that sure as hell doesn't sound like something he'd offer."

Pike rubs the back of his neck, lifting one shoulder. "He said they needed someone part time to cover the desk because you're too busy with your own customers now."

I blink, because sure, it made sense, but Austin? My dad isn't the biggest fan of Pike, and now, after Austin's outburst, I'm not sure he would even give Austin the time of day.

"I figured we'd drop by the shop, feel out your dad a bit, and see what happens from there."

I go back to my coffee, sipping slowly, thinking over all the ways this could end in disaster. I liked being there when Pike and my dad were in the same room so I could be the referee, but today it isn't possible.

"I'm going to get ready so we can go shopping, okay?" Tamara asks, interrupting my train of thought of all the horrible ways their stop by the shop could end.

"Yeah. I'll be ready in thirty," I tell her, bringing my attention back to Pike as she disappears down the same hallway Austin just went down.

"Hey, sweet cheeks," Austin says from his room, that Southern drawl coming out just a little.

"Change in Pike's room!" I yell.

Tamara and Austin burst into laughter, knowing full well they were just trying to get a rise out of me.

I fell for it too. Hook. Line. And sinker.

"You think I shouldn't go?" Pike bumps his hip into me when I don't take my eyes off the hallway, making sure both parties are separate so there're no shenanigans.

"No. Of course you should go," I lie. "What's the worst that could happen?"

Everything.

Pike smiles, nodding like he believes the bullshit coming out of my mouth. "We won't be long. We'll be back to help you carry whatever you need inside."

"It's going to be a lot," I warn him, wrapping my arms around his neck and soaking in those deep green eyes.

"Darlin', I'd carry the weight of the world on my shoulders for you."

"Which one is Morris again?" Tamara asks as we sit at lunch, trying to find more energy to keep shopping.

We've managed to buy almost everything I need for the kitchen, which isn't much because, like my mother, I suck at cooking. We bought pillows, bedding, towels, and just enough other things to make the place livable and as comfortable as a dorm room. In time, I'll make it more of a home, but for now, it would do.

"He's a guy in the Disciples. One of Pike's good friends."

Her dark brown eyebrows wrinkle as she studies me over her double burger. "So, he shot Pike in the shoulder, but they're friends?"

I know what she's thinking. It's bananas and something I'll never understand about men.

"Yep," I snap the P.

"If a bitch even looks at me sideways, I'm never going to be her friend. If she shoots me…" She shakes her head, that pile of brown hair moving with her, still not comprehending the way a man's brain works. "I'd kill her."

I shrug, shifting through my fries to find a crunchy little one. "I don't understand it, Tam, but he's really a nice guy."

She blinks at me, dropping her chin. "He's a nice guy?"

I nod. "He's super sweet and funny."

"He shot Pike," she reminds me as if I didn't just tell her that five seconds ago.

"I know, but it was on accident."

She blinks those hazel eyes again, placing her burger back on the plate. "You sound like him now. He shot Pike, but it's okay because it wasn't on purpose and he's nice."

"Uh, yeah," I say like duh.

"Where's my cousin, and what have you done with her?"

I snort, knowing I sound like a complete psycho. "Stop it." I throw a fry in her direction, one that's limp and wasn't going in my mouth anyway. "I'm just telling you what happened."

"Is Morris hot?" She lifts an eyebrow, her old-man radar going off. "'Cause he sounds badass."

"Are you out of your freaking mind?" I gawk at her.

She smirks. "You said he's funny and sweet. Plus, if he's any kind of a badass biker dude like Pike, I'm all in, baby."

I reach up and rub my temples, instantly regretting it when my greasy fingers slide across my skin. "Morris is old enough to be your father."

She grimaces but quickly rebounds. "Does he have a son?" she asks in a super chipper tone. "Because if he does—" she waggles her eyebrows "—I want to meet him."

"What is wrong with you?" I ask her, going back to pushing around my French fries.

"I need to move on with my life. What was it that Mallory told you?" She lifts a finger, staring upward, recalling those words from almost two years ago. "The best way to get over someone is to get under someone else. Maybe we can go over to the compound one night for a party."

I drop the fry from my fingers and push my entire plate to the side. Leaning forward, I whisper, "Are you out of your fucking mind?"

"No," she insists calmly. "I'm just looking for a good time, and nothing sounds like more fun than a biker party."

I close my eyes, sucking in the deepest breath, trying not to lose my shit in the middle of the restaurant. "You've watched way too much television. Biker parties are…"

"You're trying to tell me there's not dick for days?"

"Dick for days?" I giggle. "Did you just say that?"

She nods slowly, tossing her dark locks behind her shoulder. "I'm not looking for anything serious, babe. You know me. I've been in enough shit relationships to last me a while. I just want some cock, goddamn it."

The lady next to us starts choking, clearly hearing every filthy word coming out of my sweet cousin's mouth. Within seconds, she has picked up her plate and is moving across the restaurant with the plate in her hands.

"Nice," I tell her, rolling my eyes.

She shrugs. "Whatever. That lady could probably use some dick too."

"There's something seriously wrong with you," I whisper, trying to hold back my laughter. "I really missed your dumb ass."

"I missed you too." She smiles. "This is going to be the best summer ever."

Heaven help me.

13

PIKE

Austin hasn't said three words to me since we got in the truck, finding the scenery way more interesting. "We need to talk about yesterday."

He doesn't look in my direction. "I think you said enough."

I deserve the shitty attitude. I know how much words hurt, sometimes more than any fist. "I'm sorry for what I said, Austin. It was such an asshole thing to say. I didn't really mean for it to come out like that."

He lifts a shoulder. "It doesn't matter," he mutters as he rests his cheek against his palm.

"It does. It matters a hell of a lot." I flick my gaze to him, wishing he'd at least look at me, but he doesn't.

When the girls were around, he was a funny, smartass guy, but as soon as they walked out of the apartment, he went cold.

"I'm not stuck with you. I wanted you to be here with me," I admit, trying to dig myself out of the verbal grave I've been buried in since my talk with Joe. "Gran would've been more than happy to have you live with her, but I thought we'd spent enough time apart that nothing else made sense other than to bring you home."

"Yay, me," he cheers in the most unenthusiastic voice, one full of sarcasm. "I'm a lucky guy."

"I know I was an asshole," I admit.

"You always have been," he shoots back immediately.

I bite my lip, stopping myself from telling this little fucker off. "I deserve that."

He finally glances in my direction. "Even though you weren't there, I looked up to you, man. Even with all the bad shit, I was so freaking happy to see my big brother again. And what did you do?"

"I fucked up."

"Do you know how it feels when you know you aren't wanted?"

It's my turn to give him the side-eye because it's the only thing I knew as a child. Felt that shit every damn day.

He closes his eyes, knowing how he's just fucked up. "It sucks," he groans.

"I never want you to feel how Mom and—" I pause and almost say Colton, but I catch myself "—Dad made me feel every day. If I could take the words back, I would. It was the most asshole-ish thing I've ever said."

"I highly doubt that." He snorts.

Pulling into the lot of Inked, I know I have to smooth shit over before we walk inside. If Austin's on edge and a total shithead, he's only going to bury me deeper. Plus, I don't want my brother to feel unwanted, even though I didn't expect to have a seventeen-year-old living with me right now. "I know you're almost a man."

"Damn right," he blurts out.

I resist the urge to roll my eyes. "And I'm not Mom or Dad." God, that word is like acid on my tongue, burning every time I say the single syllable. "But we're in this together. I had Gran looking out for me around your age before I took off, and I want to be there for you before you do whatever it is you're going to do after this year."

He doesn't reply, just stares out the window, checking out the shop at the end of the truck's hood.

So, I keep going. "Do you want a job?"

"Do you want me to work here?" He ticks his head toward Inked, and his brown hair flops over into his eyes. "You work here, right?" he finally asks, looking at me again.

I nod, blowing out a long, long breath. "I want you here. I work a lot in the evenings, so this would be the only way for us to spend more time together."

He twists his lips and narrows his eyes, but at least I have his attention. "You mean so you can keep an eye on me."

I shake my head and grimace. "You're not a little boy. We need to get to know each other all over again, and that isn't happening when I'm working all night."

His gaze goes back to the tattoo shop, eyes sweeping over the front window and the flurry of activity inside. "What do I have to do?"

"Work the front desk, welcome customers, answer phones. Gigi used to do it, but now she has her own chair."

Austin drops his arm, straightening in the seat. "You think he'll still hire me?"

"I don't know, kid. The guy hates me."

He gives me a *no shit* look. "You are fucking his kid."

I glare at him. "Never say those words again."

"Fine." He rolls his eyes. "You're dating his daughter. Better?"

I point toward Inked. "She's related to everyone in there. Her aunt, father, and uncles own the place and work there. And I work there. If you're a shithead…"

"I know how not to be an asshole, Pike. I've had a

job since I was fifteen, and I am a damn good employee."

"Where?" I ask.

"Over at the Sanders' farm. I worked after school and on weekends to save some money for a bike."

"A bicycle?" I ask, raising my eyebrows.

He shakes his head. "I'm $1000 away from having the keys to my own Harley."

"Maybe you should get a junk car first."

He gives me the same look I gave Gran when she said the same thing to me. Jesus Christ, I am turning into an old person.

"Cars are too expensive, and I've wanted a Harley since..."

"Since I took you for a ride on mine," I reply, remembering him as a little kid with his hands wrapped around my waist, screaming at the top of his lungs as he sat on the back.

He smiles. "Yeah."

"Harley it is, then." I'm not one-hundred-percent comfortable with the idea, but who the fuck am I to tell him no?

"Can we go inside?" He reaches for the handle but doesn't open the door, waiting for me to answer.

We're not two steps inside when Mike, Gigi's uncle and the ex-fighter, steps right in front of us, locking eyes on my little brother.

Austin cranes his neck back as far as it can go,

taking in the height and width of the freakishly large man. "H-hi again," Austin stutters with wide eyes.

"You're not going to pull that again, are you?" Mike threatens more than asks, his voice deep and, as always, scary as shit.

"No, sir." Austin swallows.

A slow smile spreads across Mike's face as he places his hand on my little brother's shoulder. "You have things to work through, but you save them for when you're away from the customers and on your own time."

"Yeah," Austin whispers. "My own time."

I chuckle to myself, watching my brother virtually piss his pants as Mike squeezes his shoulder hard enough to make him wince.

"Smart kid."

"Austin," Izzy says in a singsong voice, walking quickly into the front of the shop, knocking her brother out of the way with her hip. A moment later, her arms are open and around my brother's shoulders like she's missed him.

Hell, the woman never hugged me. She's never looked at me the way she looks at him. No matter what I've done, I've never told the entire family to go fuck themselves. But here we are, and Izzy is being…motherly?

She pulls back, but her hands stay on his arms,

never breaking contact. "Are you doing okay? We were worried."

"I'm fine now, ma'am."

My eyes widen immediately, waiting for her to rip him a new asshole like she did me the first time I called her ma'am.

She laughs, slapping his arm. "It's just Iz or Izzy, kid."

He gives her a lopsided smile, probably thrown off by her hotness even if she's old enough to be his mother. "Iz," he whispers, turning a bright shade of pink but clearing his throat when it must dawn on him that he's acting like an idiot.

"Hey, Pike," Izzy throws out over her shoulder, barely even looking my way.

"Hey," I reply, rubbing the back of my neck, knowing I'm never going to get the warm and fuzzy welcome from anyone in this family.

"Joe, Austin's here." Izzy smiles at Austin, still acting like she's the sweetest thing ever. Which she isn't. "Pike too."

I walk around Izzy and Austin, heading to my chair, figuring I might as well get comfortable for a little while. I'm sure Joe's going to grill him, read him the riot act about his behavior yesterday, before making his final decision.

"Yo," Anthony murmurs, dipping his chin at me as soon as he sees me. "The girls going good?"

"They're great," I tell him. "What's going on?"

"Just waiting for them to finish so we can get out of here. I hate these monthly meetings," Anthony grumbles.

"Monthly meetings?" I raise an eyebrow, having forgotten it's Monday. When Gigi told me to take Austin to the shop today, I didn't even think about the fact that Inked was usually closed.

"Yep. All the owners meet every third Monday to talk about the financial affairs and store business. It's Mike's idea. He's such a pain in the ass."

I snort but quickly wipe that look off my face when Mike walks in the back. "What are you two bitches talking about?"

"Your meeting." Anthony kicks back, resting his feet on a nearby stool as he folds his hands behind his head. "Are we done? You've already gone on and on for almost two hours."

I grab my phone, swiping across the screen to the text app, letting them talk.

Me: Hey, darlin'. How's shopping?

"As soon as Joe's done talking to Austin, we'll leave," Mike says, dropping into a chair so hard, I'm shocked it doesn't buckle under his weight.

Gigi: Tamara's on the prowl.

Me: For dishes?

I scratch my face, staring at the screen, ignoring the two guys bickering across the room from me.

Gigi: A man!!! A badass biker man. WTF is wrong with her?

I have nothing. I don't even know how to respond to something like that.

Gigi: Other than that, it's going well. We'll be back in a few hours.

Me: We'll be ready.

"Gigi?" Mike asks, making me lift my head.

"Yeah. They're shopping."

Joe strolls into the room with Austin at his side. "We'll start training you as soon as you're ready to start working."

"I'm ready as soon as you are, sir." Austin smiles up at the big guy.

"You can work as many hours as you want until school starts, and then we'll cut back. Nothing's more important than your schoolwork."

Austin blanches for a moment before wiping that shitty look right off his face. "I agree," he lies.

I didn't even think about homework, classes, report cards, and all the shit that's involved in dealing with a seventeen-year-old. Was Austin a good student? I don't have a clue, but something tells me he wasn't on the honor roll.

Izzy walks up behind Austin, giving him a quick hug around his shoulders. "We're happy to have you as part of the family."

I should take offense. No one's given me a hug,

but fuck it. I'm not a kid, and the fact that they're so willing to open their arms and business to my brother is enough for me.

"Me too," Austin babbles, practically beaming as her tits smash against his biceps.

I climb to my feet, jamming my phone back into my pocket. "Ready to hit it?" I ask Austin, more than ready to roll.

"The girls done?" Joe asks, the smile that had been on his face vanishing as soon as he looks at me.

I nod. "They'll be headed back soon."

Joe eyes Anthony for a moment before looking at me. "Anthony and I are going to follow you back. I have a trailer filled with furniture Suzy's been storing up for this day. Beds, couches, and all that bullshit."

Anthony's on his feet, rubbing his hands together like he's ready to get moving. "Between the four of us, we should be able to at least get everything in before they get back. It'll be a nice surprise."

"I'm game," Austin exclaims, being totally agreeable and nothing like the grumpy fucker who was just in my truck. "Wanna come, Iz?"

Wanna come, Iz? It takes everything in me not to roll my eyes. The kid is such a flirt. It doesn't matter how old a woman is, he is totally going there.

"I have to pick up my sons from football practice, and then I'm meeting my husband for an early dinner. He has to work late tonight." She ruffles

Austin's hair, making him blush. "But thanks for the offer."

He bobs his head, jamming his hands into his front pockets. "Anytime."

"Mike, you comin'?" Joe asks him as he reaches into his back pocket, fishing out his cell phone.

"Can't. With Lily home, Mia wants the family to go down to the beach for dinner and to watch the sunset."

"That's so sweet. I'm dreading the day Carm and Rocco head off to college. Dreading," Izzy groans, shaking her head. "I won't know what to do with myself."

"Trace will no doubt keep you busy," Anthony tells her with a snicker. "That boy is a wild man."

She rolls her eyes. "He's like his daddy. He's going to put me in an early grave."

"We'll meet you at the apartment," I say, done with all the sugary sweetness that was the Gallo family.

Joe nods his head. "Be there in five."

"See you tomorrow," Austin tells Izzy and Mike with a wave of one hand, following me out of Inked. "I like them."

"Yeah?" I ask, sliding into the driver's seat of Gigi's pickup truck she let me borrow since they were taking Tam's car. "They're not the worst people ever."

Austin laughs, slamming the door after he settles

into the seat. "I feel awful about being such a dipshit yesterday."

"You should," I grumble, turning the ignition.

"Asshole," he mutters in response. "You ever…" He drags his hand down his face as he cranes his neck toward me, hesitating for a moment before speaking. "Ever wish we'd had a large family like that?"

I wince, not sure how to answer the question, but then I explain exactly what I feel and leave nothing out. "I wish we had a family like that." I point to the people in the shop in front of us. "Would I want a large family if they were dysfunctional like our parents?" I pause and shake my head. "No fucking way."

"I like the Gallos. I could've totally dug being in a family with those people growing up. Imagine all the birthdays, holidays… Hell…" He smiles. "Think about Christmas."

"I know, Austin. We were shortchanged, but at least we have each other now," I tell him, backing out of the parking spot.

"Can you do me a solid?" he begs, his voice suddenly serious.

"What?" I glance over at him before I put the truck in drive.

"Can you not fuck it up with Gigi for a little while so we can at least have a great Christmas this year. Okay, brother?"

I stare him straight in the eyes, but without any anger, just pure honesty. "It's a two-way street. Don't do anything like that shit," I say, referring to yesterday's performance before dinner, "and I think we have a solid chance of making the guest list."

He nods, smiling as we head off toward home.

14

GIGI

"We can't sleep here tonight," Tamara announces hours after our fathers leave. The apartment is an absolute mess.

I look around, taking in the level of mass destruction in the living room and dining room, not even wanting to peer down the hallway toward the bedrooms. "It's bad, Tam."

Boxes are everywhere in various states of unpacking, and the washer and dryer are going at full steam as the new sheets and towels we'd purchased are being cleaned. Every few feet, there's something that needs to be moved or cleaned, and absolutely nothing has been completed.

Tamara groans, collapsing on the couch. "I didn't think this would be so much work." She throws her arm over her face, being super dramatic, but I wouldn't expect anything less from her. "Moving in to a dorm room was so much easier. I can barely move another muscle."

"We can just push everything onto the floor and crash on the couches."

Her arms move upward so her hazel eyes are visible. "Do you even know where the toilet paper is?"

I glance around at the various boxes and bags scattered everywhere and shrug. "I know where the paper towels are," I say, trying to put her mind at ease that she'd at least have something to wipe her ass with.

She scowls. "My lady parts are way too sensitive for paper towels," she argues.

I snort, smacking her legs with my hand as I collapse next to her. "I know where your *lady parts* have been, and I'm pretty sure sensitive isn't a word I'd use to describe them."

"You're a bitch," she snaps, laughing with me because she knows she's full of shit. "We should totally have another sleepover with Aussie and Pike."

I roll my eyes, leaning back into the couch and pulling her legs onto my lap. "We should give them space tonight. They could use some alone time."

Now it's her turn to snort. "They need alone time?" She laughs louder, hitting my shoulder with her bony elbow, knocking me to the side. "They're not chicks. They've got dicks, dude. They don't need alone time. I can guarantee they'd love to have us over again."

I straighten, rubbing the spot she's just assaulted. "This is our first official night together in our new place."

"Fuck that," she sasses and slides her legs off me, climbing to her feet quickly. "We can have that night tomorrow. I don't want to work anymore."

She's such a whiny bitch sometimes, but I still love her. I sigh and grab a glittery pillow that's itchy as hell and not very comfortable, clutching it to my chest. "We don't have to work. Let's just veg and watch some Netflix. We'll start straightening up tomorrow. Leave the boys alone tonight."

"I gotta piss," she announces, being the classy bitch she is.

That's my Tamara.

"The paper towels are in the laundry room!" I yell to her as she marches down the hallway, stomping her feet, having her own little temper tantrum.

I pull out my phone, wondering how it's going next door since the guys left an hour ago. I haven't heard any yelling, so I assume it's going great, but after the last few days…anything could be possible.

Me: Whatcha doin'?

A second later, three dots are on the screen like Pike had been about to text me when I sent the message.

Pike: He's in his room. I'm on the couch. Fun times. You?

I glance up, taking in the chaos all around me.

Me: Tamara's giving up, and I'm tired.

Pike: Want some help?

Me: No. We got it. It's not your mess.

Pike: One sec. Austin's yelling for me.

Me: K

"Oh, Gigi!" Tamara yells from the hallway, her steps lighter than before. "Guess what?"

"Your lady bits aren't as sensitive as you thought they were?" I laugh until I see her face because I know the asshole is up to something. "What?" I groan.

She twists around, putting her hands behind her back as she stands only a few feet away from me. "The guys want us to come over. We're having another sleepover!"

"You didn't!"

"I so did," she sings, looking mighty damn pleased with herself.

"Asshole," I grumble under my breath, fisting the pillow in my hands and throwing the glittery monstrosity at her face.

She ducks, and the pillow sails past her, sliding across the tile. "Come on. You can snuggle with Pike, and we can use real toilet paper. It's a win-win."

"If I have to listen to any more Aussie and

TamTam shit…" I make a gagging sound and lean over like I'm throwing up.

"You're just jealous," she tells me, crossing her arms over her chest. "You wish you could have such cute nicknames."

I glare at her because she's unbelievable, and then my phone vibrates next to me.

Pike: Come over.

"What'd he say?" Tamara asks, stepping closer, trying to get a good look at my phone.

"We'll go. Just…" I look down at her chest, remembering this morning. "For the love of God, wear a damn sports bra."

She glances down at her tits, which are propped up by her arms. "Why?"

"Those suckers are like laser beams, and Austin's only seventeen." I motion toward her nipples, which are hard like she's perpetually cold. "He doesn't need to be seeing them."

She drops her arms and cups her breasts in the palms of her hands. "These cannot be contained. A sports bra is too constricting." She bounces her tits like she's testing their weight.

"You know what's constricting?" I glare at her.

"What?"

"My fingers wrapped around that beautiful neck of yours," I threaten.

"Fine," she says. "I'll wear a damn sports bra."

"Thank fuck," I mutter, glancing up at the ceiling. "Don't give that kid any ideas. He's young, Tam. Too young."

"We're just friends."

"You know that—" I motion toward her with my hand before smacking my own chest "—and I know that, but that horny little toad next door does not."

"They'll be locked and loaded, baby. Don't worry," she laughs, turning on her heel and stalking toward her bedroom. "I'm putting my pjs on now before we head over."

Me: We're coming. Give us five.

Pike: I'll be waiting, darlin'.

My insides go all squishy when I read *darlin',* just like they do every time he says that word.

Tam is right. Spending the night curled up with Pike is so much better than sitting in the middle of this disaster, listening to her whine all night.

Ten minutes later, we're on Pike's couch, my legs curled up against me and my back to his front. Tamara and Austin are on the floor, legs stretched out, looking like the oddest set of twins.

"Nope," Austin tells her, grabbing the remote from her hands. "You ladies picked last night. It's guys' night."

Tamara pulls the remote back toward her, but Austin doesn't let go. "That's bullshit. We're your guests."

Austin blinks but doesn't give in. "You asked to come here, babe, not the other way around."

Snap. He shut her down good.

Her eyes narrow, and she doesn't say a word before pulling back, causing Austin to lean forward. And then, like the asshole she is, she lets go, making him fall on her. "Whatever, bitch," she tells him.

I glance up at Pike as he gazes down at me with those pretty eyes. "I hate them," I mouth.

"Me too," he mouths back.

"Shut up, ass." Austin lifts himself upward but not before totally checking out her rack.

Gross.

"Eyes there," she reminds him, pushing his face toward the television. "Unless you don't want to be able to see out of them for a week."

He scrunches his nose. "They're not that amazing, TamTam. They were in my face, for Christ's sake."

Telling Tamara her tits aren't *the shit* is like saying her face is ugly. Those are fighting words. Seventeen or not, he will pay for that remark.

She lets out this loud growl, rearing her arm back like she's going to sock him right in the face. But Austin flinches, and Tamara instantly breaks out in giggles, pointing at him. "Sucker," she snorts.

"I hate you sometimes," he grumbles, lifting the remote toward the television.

"No, you don't." She smiles as she stares at the screen.

"We're watching *Aquaman,* and I don't want any lip," he tells her, sounding all serious.

Watching that movie is not going to be a hardship. In fact, Tamara has said she'd climb Jason Momoa like a tree on more than one occasion. She even had a poster of him above her bed in her dorm room.

"Shut up!" she screeches, clapping her hands like she just heard the best news ever. "Jason Momoa is a total dreamboat."

"If you like old dudes," Austin grumbles, pressing the button to start the movie.

I settle into Pike as he wraps his arms around my middle and his lips move to my neck. Closing my eyes, I moan softly as the wet warmth of his mouth connects with my skin, sending goose bumps pebbling down my arms.

I turn my face, placing my mouth so close to his lips, I can feel his warm breath. "Stop," I plead, the tingle between my legs making me wish we weren't saddled with the two assholes still grumbling at each other on the floor like they're brother and sister.

"Shh," he whispers, his warm breath skidding across my skin, using his nose against my jaw to push my face back toward the television.

My body stiffens as he places his mouth near my

ear, his breath tickling my flesh and turning that tingling into a full-on throb.

"Let me enjoy your skin," he pleads in such a husky tone, my body shivers before I can stop it. "Just be still, and no one will ever know what we're doing."

I instantly lift up my hand, pulling a nearby blanket on top of us. "Man, I'm so cold," I say because I'm lame.

Tamara looks back, eyes raking over us before she winks and turns back toward the television. It's not the first time we've been in the same room together when one of us was literally necking. That's the bitch about college… There's zero privacy.

"Who's your favorite superhero?" Tamara asks Austin as the opening credits are just about to finish.

"Iron Man. You?"

"Aquaman all day, bitch."

I tune them out as Pike's hand slides down my front, resting on my stomach. My breath hitches as his mouth attaches to that spot near my shoulder that always makes it impossible to breathe.

Pike's cock presses into my back, straining against his sweat pants and making me pant. I want him so damn bad.

"Think we could sneak out without them knowing?" Pike whispers when I shift, and his cock twitches right above my ass cheeks.

I shake my head, unable to speak without sounding like a needy whore.

"Damn," he hisses. "This is going to be the longest movie of my life."

I giggle, my body shaking as Pike growls, pulling his bottom away from my back.

"We gotta stop," he bites out softly. "Or I'm going to die."

I pull myself forward, putting as much space between us as possible. "Stay over there," I mouth to him, kicking my feet into his lap.

He scowls as he wraps his long, strong fingers around my feet and rubs, causing me to moan loudly.

Austin turns his head, eyes flickering at Pike's fingers on my feet and grimaces. "Weirdo," he mutters before turning back around.

Pike winks at me, and all I can do is laugh.

I don't know when I fall asleep, but I am awakened when strong hands slide under my bottom, lifting me into a pair of warm arms. My face flops into the warm muscles of his chest, and I groan, hating the idea I'd be left on the cold couch without Pike to keep me warm.

"Off to bed?" Tamara whispers.

I don't even have the energy to reply, but Pike does. "I'm taking her with me. You two behave," he commands ever so quietly to Tamara and Austin before taking another step, holding me firmly in his grasp.

I don't open my eyes until he places my body on the cool sheets of his bed and covers me with his body heat.

"I've been waiting all night for this," he whispers in the darkness, his face level with mine. "All fucking night to taste you."

A lazy smile stretches across my face as I spread my legs. "Taste away."

He crawls down my body, placing soft kisses on my skin, giving equal love to each breast. I moan, shoving my fingers into his hair as he sucks my nipple between his lips.

"Quiet," he murmurs around my flesh, reminding me of the two in the living room.

The warmth of his mouth is gone, and then the hard muscles of his shoulders slide between my legs, opening me to him.

Pike studies my skin in the faint light. "You're so beautiful," he whispers, glancing up at my face for a moment.

I push his face down, done with the compliments, needing his mouth back on my body. The coolness from the room is replaced by the damp heat of his tongue, causing my hips to jolt off the bed.

He hums his approval and wraps his hands around my thighs, stopping me from squirming.

When his lips close around my flesh, I moan loudly, throwing my hand over my mouth to stop the sound.

Pike doesn't stop, sucking harder and rubbing his tongue over the perfect spot.

"Yes," I moan into my palm. "Oh my God."

Another moan escapes as Pike's lips send vibrations through my system, making my toes curl.

"I'm going to come," I whisper, biting down on my lip.

His fingers are at my opening, pushing inside and stretching me. Just when I don't think the pleasure could get better, goose bumps break out across my flesh.

This is it. I can't stop the wave of pleasure from crashing over me again and again, building in intensity with each thrust of his long, thick fingers inside me.

I gasp for air, my body growing rigid as the orgasm takes over, making it impossible to even think. I rock forward, possessed by the passion only his lips can deliver.

"Goddamn," he whispers as he pulls away, and I collapse back into the mattress. "That was too quick."

"I'm sorry." I smile, too sated to care how fast or slow I came.

"Let's do that again, but slower this time." He grins, placing those lips back on my skin.

Damn, I love this man.

15

PIKE

Morris: 8 pm at the Neon Cowboy

I flick my eyes to my phone, reading over the message a second time before I look up. *Shit.* They're here. James and Thomas said they'd come. The Disciples wanted payback.

Me: I'll be there

I type the message, hitting send before I have a chance to think. If I had taken a minute, or hell, a few seconds, I would've remembered James's words.

I had forgotten they were coming. Days had passed. Night turned into day, bleeding into almost a week before Morris had finally reached out to me.

Morris: Bring the sweetheart with you

"Who are you talking to?" Gigi asks as we sit in the living room at her grandmother's house.

It's Sunday. Family day. It's the weekly celebration

of everything Gallo. Austin's been welcomed back as if last weekend never happened.

"Morris," I mutter softly, trying to avoid the attention of everyone else in the room.

Gigi's eyes widen as soon as his name is off my lips. "We should tell..."

I touch her hand, stopping her from saying any more. I know the protocol. The last thing I'm going to do is fuck things up with this family again.

I get to my feet and lean over to kiss her cheek. "I'll be back. Let me talk to the guys," I whisper in her ear, earning me a quick nod.

I catch James's eye, motioning toward the dining room with my head, and he slaps Thomas's shoulder before they both are right behind me.

"Disciples reach out?" James asks as soon as we're in the dining room, far away from the rest of the family.

"Yeah. Neon Cowboy tonight." I tap my knuckles against the table, the muscles across my shoulders already growing tight. "He wants me to bring Gigi."

James looks at Thomas, unspoken words passing in their gazes. Thomas and James slide into the chairs across from me, looking calm and collected like I didn't just tell them that payback was on the horizon.

"What do I do?" I ask, flexing my fingers, trying to contain my nervous energy.

Thomas rubs his chin, studying me. "If they want

Gigi to come along, most likely, they'll tell you what the favor is, but it won't happen tonight."

"Are you sure?" I ask, my voice serious and deep. "What if she's part of the favor?"

James's eyebrows shoot up. "Fuck no," he howls quickly. "You know these guys. They wouldn't ask for her. They know they'd have to go through all three of us, and then I'd rain down fire upon them."

I nod immediately, knowing Tiny, Morris, and everyone in the Disciples as well as I've known anyone in my life. "They wouldn't."

"Take her," Thomas orders. "Don't stay too long. Keep shit short and simple. Do not, and I mean do not, go anywhere with them without calling us first."

"We're not fucking around, Pike," James barks like I'm an idiot and can't follow directions.

"I'm not a dumbass," I bite back.

James narrows his eyes and flattens his lips. "Call us from the Neon, and don't be an asshole."

"Who's going to the Neon?" Joe asks, eavesdropping.

The man has been so far up my ass for the last week. I'm surprised he doesn't have a drone following me around, making sure I'm not fucking up somehow.

"Pike and Gigi are just going for drinks later," Thomas tells him, leaving out the most important information.

I close my eyes because why couldn't the man just

say I was going alone. Joe didn't need to know everything. What the hell is wrong with this family? Can't anyone do something without everyone being up one another's asses?

That would be a hard no.

Joe's arms are down at his sides, hands fisted tightly, probably dreaming about punching me right between the eyes. "Tonight?" he growls.

"They're meeting Morris," James offers, climbing to his feet as soon as Joe moves forward like he's going to land that punch. "Hold up, big guy. It's not a big deal. Morris saved her life, remember." James blocks Joe from reaching me.

Joe swings his eyes from James, to me, to Thomas before landing back on James. "It is a big fucking deal. This is my kid we're talking about, and they are —" his eyes go stone-cold, jaw tightening as he glares at me "—criminals."

If looks could kill, I'd be a dead man. Hell, I would've been good and buried, my body rotting in the ground by now. "I'll keep her safe," I tell him, trying to smooth shit out because the last thing I need is more trouble.

"If she's going, I'm going," he demands.

Thomas lets out a loud laugh. "Yeah, 'cause everyone wants their daddy to tag along."

The shade of red on Joe's face matches that of the spaghetti sauce I'd just shoved down my throat.

"Would you let your daughter go alone?" Joe pauses, staring his brother down. "Oh, wait. You have a fucking son."

Thomas isn't thrown off by his brother's anger. "Fine." Thomas throws up his hands. "We'll all go. We'll gather the ALFA guys and sit at our usual table so we can keep an eye on them. How's that, big guy?"

I shake my head, knowing immediately this entire evening is going to be nothing but a giant clusterfuck. The biggest epic failure. Dread washes over me, coating my skin and clinging to my back like a second shirt.

"Sounds like a great time," I mutter to the table as I rub my forehead with my fingers. "Fan-fucking-tastic."

"Hey, dipshit," Joe heckles, and I know he's talking to me.

I glance up, looking at him straight on. "What?" I growl because I've had just about enough of his shit.

"That bar used to be my bar. I know exactly what happens in a place like that, and I'm not letting you take my kid in there to meet the Disciples without being nearby."

"Where am I going?" Gigi asks, standing behind her father, appearing out of nowhere just like he did.

There's seriously not a room in this house with any privacy. Even if you think you've found a spot, someone will show up, reminding you just how public everything is and how nosy they all are.

"Pike—" Joe motions toward me "—is taking you to the Neon Cowboy tonight to meet Morris." He says the words in such a shitty way, like I'm taking her to the worst place imaginable.

Gigi's eyes light up, and she practically jumps in the air. "Oh my God. I freakin' love Morris." Her body's humming with excitement about seeing the old guy again. "He's such a hoot."

There's no happiness on Joe's face. "Jesus Christ," he mutters, glancing upward toward the ceiling. "Have you all lost your minds?"

"Daddy." Gigi smiles up at him. "You know you like Morris."

"I put up with him. Like is too strong of a word."

The bastard doesn't even like me, and I almost died for his kid. I'm pretty sure I'd actually have to take that bullet before he'd let go of that chip on his shoulder. But then again, probably not.

"We're all going," Thomas tells Gigi, and I wince, closing an eye because I know my girl, and she's going to…

"Like hell you are," she bellows, hands going to her hips and eyes burning with fire. "You are not going to embarrass me."

"We would never do that, baby girl."

Gigi cranes her neck, glaring up at her father.

"You are not going. Neither are they." She tips her head toward her uncles but never breaks eye contact with Joe. "I've put up with your overprotective nonsense for my entire life." She lifts her hand, pushing her fingertip into his chest. "I will not do it anymore."

He glances down at where their bodies are touching but doesn't otherwise move. "You're not going alone," he tells her.

Gigi lets out a loud, dramatic groan. "I won't be alone. I'm going with Pike, and Jesus Christ, stop being so mean to him. He's kind, loving, and an over-protective jerk just like you, so lay off."

My gaze moves to Joe's face, and he's eyeing me, anger coming off him in waves.

"No one will keep you as safe as I would," Joe replies, barely moving his lips as he speaks.

He's about to blow. No man talks without moving his mouth unless he's so mad, he's about to beat someone to death. I'd sure as hell be the victim, but I'd put up one hell of a fight before I took my last breath.

"You know you have two other daughters and a wife, right?" she throws back, not missing a beat. "I'm sure one of them needs your protection. I have Pike, Daddy." She pulls her fingers back before sliding her palm against her father's chest. "I love you with all my heart. You're the best father a girl could ever want. I won the lottery the day I was born, getting you and Mom as parents. But, Dad…" She curls up against him, looking so small against the big man. "You have to let go sometime. Pike will never replace you. I love you, and I love him."

Joe's eyes cut to me, first hard. But then, like something comes over him, they soften for a moment. "You love him?" He sounds like he's choking on those words.

She peers up, nodding. "I love him, and I love you," she tells him again. "Just let go, Daddy. Let me grow up and find my own way. You taught me well. I know how to be safe and not be stupid, and when all else fails, Pike will be there."

"Goddamn it," Joe mutters, curling his arm around his daughter's back. "I never thought this would be so hard."

"I'll always be your little girl, but you have to let me live my own life too," she pleads, embracing her father, head still on his chest. "I promise I'll make you proud."

"Sweetheart," he whispers, kissing the top of her head. "You already make me so damn proud. I love you more than anything else in the world."

"More than Mom?" Gigi asks, teasing her father, because the girl always has to bust balls.

Three hours later, Gigi's under my arm as we walk into the Neon Cowboy, a bar I've only been to a handful of times since I moved to the area. It's your typical country biker bar with loud music, cold beer, and not much else.

Gigi's talk with her father convinced him and her uncles to give us space. I swore on my life that I'd keep her safe, and if I didn't, I expected to pay with my own life.

"There she is," Morris says, pushing his body away from the bar the moment he sees Gigi. "Beautiful as always, sweetheart." He holds out his arms to her like he's her long-lost father, and my girl, she just runs to him.

"I've missed you," she tells him, giving him the biggest bear hug as he lifts her feet off the floor, reciprocating.

Fuck me.

"Pike," he mumbles, still hugging on her and barely glancing in my direction.

"Let her go, Morris," I tell him, and not in that *hey, how you doin'* kind of tone either. When he just looks at me, pretending he didn't hear every word out of my mouth, I reach out and grab her arm, hauling her back against me.

"Don't be a buzzkill," is her response, as she throws a glare over her shoulder at me, shrugging out of my grip. "So." She hooks her arm around his and starts walking to where Morris left his beer. "What's new with all my badass biker friends?"

I walk behind them, reminding myself not to lose my cool. This is Gigi being Gigi. She's going to test my limits, and in all reality, Morris hasn't done a goddamn thing. *He saved our lives.* It's something I reminded myself of a hundred times on the way over here. Nothing will happen to us. Not after everything the MC lost to protect us.

"After you two left and the smoke cleared, we swore in some new members." Morris motions toward the bartender, holding out three fingers and pointing toward the spot in front of him.

Gigi's eyebrows go up. "Really?"

"Yeah. You'll have to come celebrate with us and meet the new guys. We're having a huge party on Labor Day weekend if you want to come."

Like hell.

"Hell yeah," she exclaims, answering for both of us as she grabs the beer the bartender has set down for her.

"Darlin'." I slide next to her, placing my hand on the bar next to her, leaning my body against her. "We have plans with your family on Labor Day."

She looks at me over her shoulder with a straight-as-fuck face. "No, we don't," she argues. "We're going to the compound, baby."

I curl my fingers around the wooden edge of the bar, and I grind my teeth, trying to keep myself from losing my shit. *Stay calm, Pike. Breathe.*

"We'll be there. Can I bring two guests?" she asks Morris excitedly.

"No," I snap, as Morris says, "Yes."

Gigi grabs her beer, lifting it toward Morris, ignoring me again. "We'll be there, old man," she says, waiting for him to clink his beer to hers.

"It's a date." He winks, hitting her glass before lifting his to his lips.

I'm almost foaming at the mouth. What the fuck just happened? I promised her father I'd keep her safe. I promised James and Thomas we wouldn't go anywhere or do anything before I spoke to them. And Gigi just blew it all up in a matter of sixty seconds. Invitation given and accepted without so much as a moment's thought of all the ways shit could go wrong.

"Clusterfuck," I mutter.

She turns her head again and blinks. "What's your issue?" she whispers.

"Don't have an issue," I tell her after glancing up at Morris, who's watching me like a hawk. "No issue at all. Just don't want to disappoint your family."

"They won't miss us. It's two months away, damn it."

That's all she says before giving Morris her full attention again. I lift the beer to my lips, muttering a slew of curse words against the glass. I warned her about the Disciples. Did my best to tell her they're looking for payback and Morris was here to collect.

She blew me off, telling me I was imagining shit because there's no way *the big guy* would expect anything from me.

Absolutely clueless.

"I'm not bringing Austin," I tell her.

Morris's eyes widen. "You have your brother?"

I nod. "Brought him back with me after the funeral."

"No shit," Morris mutters, shaking his head, setting his beer down on the bar like he's in shock. "Didn't think you'd take him in."

"He's my family," I tell him, but Morris knows me as well as anyone. He knows family hasn't meant shit to me in the past. Why would it? They never gave two fucks about me.

"You're changing, softening," he explains, but without any judgment in his voice. His gaze dips to Gigi and then back to me. "The girl's changing you."

Gigi punches his arm playfully. "*The girl* has a name."

"I know, beautiful," he teases, throwing her a wink, and she eats that shit right up. "He stayin' forever?"

I nod, tightening my one arm around Gigi's middle, plastering my front to her back. "Never had much of a family, Morris, and now…" I flick my gaze down as Gigi looks up. "Now, I have people I love and care about in my life, and I'm not turning my back on them for nothing or no one."

Morris doesn't even twitch. The fucker is made of stone. "I can see that," he says in an even tone.

"Can you two excuse me for a moment?" Gigi asks, dipping out of my grip. "I need to use the…" She throws her thumb over her shoulder. I nod, thankful to get Morris alone.

"What the fuck?" I hiss as soon as she's far enough away. "Coming here for payback and then inviting us for a party?"

He shrugs like it's no big fucking deal. "Just because I'm here out of duty for the club doesn't mean we're not still friends."

I take a step closer to him, pushing away my beer. "You were supposed to be my friend first. I didn't think you'd come for payback for saving my life."

He nods, elbow on the bar, leaning against the edge. "Sure as fuck gotta. We lost a lot of men that night. It's going to take us a while to get back to earning what we were before that shit with DiSantis."

"I don't have any money."

Morris smiles, slow and lazy. "I heard your pops broke in to Gigi's apartment, almost killed her."

I blink, shocked he knows what's happening over here, but I shouldn't be. Just like the cops, the MC knows everything. They have eyes and ears all over the state, from dirty cops to other bikers looking for an opportunity.

"Had my guy on the inside have a little talk with your pops. He was looking for something." Morris strokes his chin, studying me. "Looking for something really important."

"I don't have any of his shit," I spit out, wondering how I ever could've thought Morris was a friend.

He reaches out, and I lurch backward, avoiding his touch. "I'm not going to hurt you or your girl. I love you like my own son, and that one—" he lifts his chin in the direction Gigi walked "—is the best thing that's ever happened to you."

"Then why the fuck are you here?"

"Word on the street is that your father has a storage locker filled floor to ceiling with cocaine and cash. The dumbass told my buddy on the inside he would split it with him if he'd find someone to track you down and get the fucking key."

"I don't have his fucking key," I grind out. The man never gave me anything besides misery.

"He hid it," Morris explains, resting his hand on my shoulder. "In some small box that was your grandfather's. I guess he put it in the box years ago. After your mother was killed, he figured he would get the key from you and cash in enough coke to live the rest of his life somewhere off the grid."

"Motherfucker," I mutter, realizing he hadn't been after Gigi, but the key and me instead. I have no doubt he would've killed me to get his hands on that key. No fucking doubt at all.

"The assholes who killed your mom," Morris says, pausing for a moment until I narrow my eyes. "They were after the key too."

I suck in a breath, knowing my brother went through hell, almost dying at the hands of the same men. Over what? Fucking drugs.

"You going to have that hanging over your head forever? Do you want to unload that kind of inventory and risk the beautiful thing you're starting with your girl?"

"Fuck no," I howl, squeezing my hand in a tight fist, wishing I could punch something…anything.

"You know which box I'm talking about?"

I nod.

Morris tightens the grip on my shoulder. "Find the key, give it to me, and we'll call it even."

"I don't fucking want it, but…" I peer up at him, looking him right in the eyes. "But if you're going to help Colton with the money…"

Morris shakes his head and barks out a laugh. "That bastard can rot in jail, kid. Fuck him. He doesn't deserve anything more than the dry ass-fucking he's going to get for the next twenty years."

The visual, while gross, brings a smile to my face.

"Bring the key, and we're even. I don't want anything else from you. I'd never hurt you or Gigi, but the longer you have the key, the more danger you'll be in. There're eyes and ears everywhere," Morris warns, knocking his knuckles against the table to drive the point home.

"I'll bring it to you," I promise.

16

PIKE

"I DON'T KNOW why I couldn't come alone." I stare out of the blacked-out windows in the back of the SUV, annoyed and aggravated that I couldn't deliver the key by myself.

"We told you. You're not going alone. Disciples or not, that's not how things are done in this family," Joe says at my side.

"It's just a simple drop," I argue.

Never in my life have I needed babysitters. I did as I was asked. I told James and Thomas exactly what Morris, Tiny, and the Disciples wanted as payback. A key that led to probably millions of dollars of illegal drugs and cash. All of it gained through violence and death, and nothing I wanted or needed.

The fact that they threw a fit when I said I was going alone was laughable. I should've taken off on my bike, delivering the key to the MC days ago. But no. That's not how this family rolls. They do everything in packs like wolves.

James grunts. "Pike, you need to start dealing with the fact that you're no longer alone in anything you do."

I glance up, meeting his eyes in the rearview mirror. "There wasn't a need for this to be a family affair," I grumble, resting my chin on my knuckles as the trees swish by so quickly, they're a blur of green.

I've always been alone. It's how I've operated from the time I was a little boy. I am used to looking out for myself, not worrying about anyone else around me.

"There's always a need," Thomas tells me, turning his neck to glower at me over his shoulder from the front seat.

"Gallos don't go into danger without backup," Joe adds with a straight face, as serious as a heart attack.

"But I'm not a…"

"Shut your mouth," Bear barks in my ear, squished into the third row of seats and sitting directly behind me. "Just say thank you, dumbass."

"Thank you," I grind out, not feeling the words but not looking to have Bear smack me in the back of the head either.

"You're welcome," Joe tells me, probably loving the shit out of my misery.

"We're five minutes out, but the Disciples are

running behind. Morris said they ran into some shit but will be there in twenty," Thomas announces.

"Fucking bikers," James groans.

"Watch it now," Bear growls under his breath. "We're not all dipshits."

I respect the hell out of every man in this SUV. They've come to my rescue before, setting aside whatever's going on in their lives to help. They never asked for anything in return and haven't given me too much shit—besides Joe. That's more than anyone in my family has ever done for me.

"Keep your eyes out as we get closer," James warns, scanning the sides of the dirt road at the endless trees.

"You think we're being set up?" Thomas asks, looking out the side window, eyes trained on the brush.

"No, but something doesn't feel right," he admits, slowing the SUV as we get closer.

Those words are enough to set off alarm bells. Thomas and James have been in more shit than I'll ever be able to fully comprehend.

"Get locked and loaded," Bear orders, the familiar sound of the metal of his gun clicking behind me.

I glance toward the ceiling, shaking my head. "What a shitshow. This is why I should've come alone."

That statement earns me a backhand to my

chest. "Stop with your bullshit already. If something's off, it's best we're all here to make it out alive, rather than sending your ass in there to get killed."

"What do you care?" I mutter, glancing over at Gigi's father, who's done nothing but hassle me since the moment he found out I'd slept with her.

Joe sucks in a breath, his blue eyes narrowing as he runs his hand through his dark hair. "I deserve that. I've been an asshole to you on more than one occasion."

"Ya think?" I raise an eyebrow, peering at him out of the corner of my eye.

"Put yourself in my shoes, kid. The last thing I want is for my girl to be staring down the barrel of a gun."

"Me either, Joe. I've told you that. I'll do everything I can to protect Gigi."

He nods. "I know, and I believe you. But I'm also not going to hold my little girl in my arms as she cries because her boyfriend had to be a goddamn hero and take a bullet when he could've made it back alive with our help."

I swallow, thinking about dying and how Gigi would react. "I don't ever want to be the cause of her tears," I tell him.

"Then we do this together."

I nod when he glares at me, waiting for some kind

of affirmation that I'd heard him. "Understood," I mutter.

James pulls the SUV over near the same spot in the abandoned parking lot where they dropped Gigi and me when the shit with DiSantis was about to go down. Night is coming, the navy skies are moving toward us with each passing second, casting shadows in the trees and the fields surrounding the patch of cement.

James cuts the engine, turning around in his seat to face us. "Don't let your guard down. Guns out, but keep them tucked in your waistband and be ready for anything."

"Shit can never be easy," Joe groans.

"I live for this shit," Bear brags with a hint of laughter, which makes him seem all the crazier than I've always thought he was.

Joe turns his head, giving Bear the glare he'd just been giving to me. "We're not as old as you, fucker. We're not looking to die today."

"I ain't dying, fool. I'm like Iron Man. The bullets bounce off." Bear pounds on his chest, trying to prove his manhood.

God, I really love these crazy assholes. They are so much like the guys in the Disciples, minus the drugs, whores, and constant partying, of course.

Joe rolls his eyes. "I don't even know why we're friends, Bear."

"You love me," Bear teases, letting his crazy show even more because shit's about to get real. "And we're not just friends. I'm your uncle."

I chuckle to myself, but my laughter dies when Joe cranes his neck and turns those hardened eyes on me.

"I need out. I gotta piss," Bear grumbles, pushing between us as he moves to my row, reaching for the door handle as he leans over me.

"Don't," James starts to tell him, but Bear's out of the SUV, almost kicking me in the junk in the process. "Goddamn him."

"Prostate," Bear mutters before the sound of his zipper followed by a loud sigh are the only noises besides the birds squawking in the distance. "You'll understand when you're older."

"Everyone out." Thomas opens his door, boots touching the gravel, creating a cloud of smoke. "Eyes peeled."

I step out, ignoring Bear as he moans, doing his business near the tire of the SUV.

"If you get piss on my tire, I'm going to make you lick it off." James stares at Bear's back, shaking his head and snarling.

"Don't worry, Sally. I'm in complete control," Bear tells him, swaying his body from side to side, fucking with James and always looking to get a rise out of everyone.

James moves to the front of the truck, leaving

Bear to finish his business. "Fuck you and your Sally shit."

"It's quiet," Thomas whispers, scanning the trees in the distance. "Too quiet."

Joe's eyes are on me as we make our way to the front of the truck to join Thomas and James. We're all on high alert, except for Bear. The man is perpetually doing his own thing, not giving a single fuck about anything else around him.

There's movement to the right, and our four sets of eyes follow, drawing out guns. This isn't the Disciples. There was no roar of their engines, no familiar rumble in the ground below our feet.

Our guns are drawn, raised out in front of us as a small army of men clears the trees with their guns drawn too.

"Fuck," I hiss softly, locking my arms straight out, drifting slightly from side to side, not sure where to point my gun.

There're so many of them. At least two dozen to our five. We're completely outnumbered, and my stomach plummets, knowing there's a strong chance we're not getting out of here.

This is my fault. The bullshit of my family is following me, spilling over onto the only family that's shown me any love.

"Goddamn it," Thomas fumes, eyes locked on the men advancing through the field.

"What do we do?" Joe asks, gun out in front of him like the rest of us.

My heart's pounding, slamming into my chest like it's trying to escape. My palms are sweating, but my hands remain steady because this isn't the first time I've been in this fucked-up situation.

"Um, guys," Bear calls out with a quiver in his voice.

"Shut up, Bear," James growls, not bothering to turn around.

We don't have time for Bear's antics. This shit is life or death. There are dozens of guns filled with hundreds of bullets, waiting to draw blood.

"Put your guns down," a voice threatens from behind us, coming from Bear's direction.

Thomas turns his head, and his eyes immediately narrow. "Goddamn it, Bear."

"This is no time for games," James barks, turning his body and gun in a semicircle because we're no doubt surrounded.

The hair on the back of my neck stands up, and my arm tenses, finger tightening on the trigger. *Stay calm.* Gigi's words, words she's told me so many times, float through my head.

"Put your guns down," the man warns again, but closer and louder than before.

"Guns!" Thomas yells out, still facing Bear, back to the others making their way toward us. "They have

Bear."

"We don't want to hurt anyone. We're only here for the kid," the man behind me explains.

I turn, knowing they want only me.

I'm the kid.

I'm the one they're after.

The men at my side, Gigi's family, are innocent in this entire thing. They never should've been here, but I let them talk me into the pack mentality, believing it was better to come in numbers than breeze into the Disciples' compound on my own.

"I'm here," I grit out, dropping my arm and the gun at my side because if they want me, they can have me. "Let him go."

The man at Bear's side has a gun to his head, snarling at me as his beady eyes land on my face. "I knew you were a pussy."

I take a step forward, holding out my arms, letting the gun twirl around my finger before it falls to the ground. "Let him go, and you can have me," I beg, somehow keeping my voice calm.

"No!" Joe yells out, stepping in front of me, blocking my movement with his back.

"What are you doing?" I yell as my stomach rolls. "They want me, Joe. I'm not worth losing your life."

"Shut up, kid," Joe barks back, not moving a muscle and not lowering the gun.

This is so fucked up. More fucked up than I ever

could've imagined. How would I go back to Gigi and explain her father died because of me? She'd never forgive me. Never love me again. No matter what, she is a daddy's girl, loving this man more than anything else in her life.

I place my hand on his shoulder, squeezing gently. "You have too much to live for. Don't be a fool," I whisper, my voice cracking because, goddamn, no one has ever stuck their neck out like this for me before.

He's rock solid, frozen and not moving. "You can't go."

"We have thirty guys to your five and another thirty waiting behind. You really want to die today?" the asshole with the gun to Bear's head asks.

No. I'm not into dying today or any day soon, but I definitely am not into letting these men, the ones I've grown to respect, die for me today either.

I stalk next to Joe, glancing at him, pleading with him with my eyes. "Let me do this, Joe. You have a wife and kids to think about. I'm not worth it. Your life isn't worth the trouble my family has brought here and has always given me."

There's a softness to Joe's blue eyes as he studies me, jaw tight with anger. "If they take you…"

I touch his arm, knowing I need to get these words out because I may not have another chance. "I'd rather they take me than you. I love your daughter. Love her more than my life, but I can't let you take a bullet for me. I can't leave her and the rest of your family knowing I was the reason we died today. Not when I can do something to stop it. I'm willing to give my life for her, for you, and for them." I angle my neck backward. "Just tell her I'm sorry and that I love her."

Joe sighs, pain written all over his face as his clenched jaw pulses. "We'll figure this out."

I push down, making him drop his hand. "I'll figure this out. Just make sure the girls and my brother are safe."

"If anything…" he says, and his voice cracks, "… happens to you, we'll make sure Austin is taken care of."

His words give me solace and a sense of peace. I never thought I'd live to be this old. I figured I was dying that day Morris put a bullet in my shoulder. I've been living on borrowed time, and now it's up. My card is being punched, but at least I won't take my last breath for no reason. I'll be saving four men, returning them to their families to keep on living and loving.

"I'll go with you, but only if you leave them be!" I yell, holding out my hands at my sides again, showing I mean no harm.

"Goddamn it," Thomas groans.

The man with the greasy hair, Viper cut, and

grizzly beard ticks his head toward the SUV. "The kid is ours, and so is everything that comes with him."

No one moves. It's like they're frozen to the ground, unsure what they should do. This is their time to run. Their way to escape. Their fucking freedom.

"Let me go!" I yell, turning to face three shocked faces, wide-eyed and ready for a gunfight. "Please. I beg you. Just leave. Go home. Go back to your family."

"You're lucky we don't want your head instead, Thomas. We know what you did to the Sun Devils. You're a traitor and a snitch. If he—" the man dips his head toward me "—wasn't so valuable, we'd be coming for you instead."

Did Morris sell us out? Would he do that? He's told me time and time again I'm like the son he never had but always wanted.

"Goddamn Morris and Tiny," James growls, thinking exactly what I am.

"Take him," Bear tells the guy still pressing the end of the gun to his head. Bear raises his hands higher in the air, and I'm praying like fuck he doesn't pull his Iron Man bullshit, thinking about getting cute and hitting the guy.

The man pushes Bear forward and motions for me with his gun. I look back, trying to give Joe a smile. "Tell her I did this for her," I plead before taking a step toward what I know will be certain death.

He nods with a scowl, not saying another word.

I step forward, head held high, walking forward without regret. I saved the life of four men today and sacrificed myself for so many others.

17

GIGI

I COVER MY MOUTH, holding back the bile that's climbing up my throat and the cry threatening to break free.

They took Pike.

The words my father uttered on speakerphone replay in my mind on an endless loop, taunting me.

"You better not come home without him," Mom whispers into the phone, peering over at me before turning her back.

They took Pike.

Rocking back and forth, I whisper to myself, "He's going to be okay. He has to be okay."

Pike always finds a way out of trouble. He has his entire life. Why would this time be any different?

The drop was supposed to be simple. At least that's what they told me when they said I couldn't go.

I should've known better.

I should've begged to be there.

It wouldn't have been the first time I faced danger, but at least I would've been there, and things could have been different.

"What's the plan?" Mom asks as I start to hyperventilate, unable to stop myself as I can't get the air into my lungs easily.

They took Pike.

My vision blurs as tears fill my eyes, and the bile in my throat inches higher.

Pike's going to… I shake my head, not allowing myself to think the worst.

"That's so dangerous," Mom whispers, looking over her shoulder at me again and grimacing.

"Oh my God," I groan, running toward the bathroom, hand clamped against my lips before everything escapes all over my mother's hardwood floor.

I lift up the seat, throwing myself over the top, and open my mouth, letting whatever's coming work its way out. I groan as my chest heaves and my stomach lurches, the nerves taking over and rationality leaving my body with it.

Tears stream down my face, plopping into the bowl and splashing as I pull away.

This is it.

This is what it feels like when you're in love with someone and you know their life is going to end. I won't get to say any final words, reminding him of how I feel. How I'll always feel.

My mother walks into the bathroom, dropping to the floor next to me, her knees hitting the marble tile. "Baby, your daddy wants to talk to you."

I take the phone, and then she grabs a hand towel, wiping my lips like I'm a baby. "Daddy," I croak, unable to keep the panic from my voice. "What happened? Where's Pike?"

"Baby girl." My father's always calm, deep timbre comes through the speaker. "I don't know how it happened, but there were other men there. But don't worry, sweetheart, we're going to find him."

Don't worry?

"Oh my God," I whisper as the tears continue to fall because my father's words aren't making me feel any better.

"We're with Morris and the Disciples, making a plan. I promise, baby." His voice cracks, and I know he's tearing up, something my father rarely does, "I swear to God, I'll bring Pike back to you."

I know my father. I know he's a man of his word, but he's not Superman. "You don't know that," I snap, my anxiety and sorrow getting the better of me.

My dad blows out a breath, no doubt feeling the weight of my pain. "I'll do everything in my power to make it happen."

"How did this go so wrong?" I wipe the tears

away from my cheeks and glance at the phone. "I thought Pike said this would be easy."

"Nothing's ever easy, baby. Especially when you're dealing with criminals." He pauses as I sniffle, feeling a fresh wave of tears coming on. "The men would've killed us all if it weren't for Pike, baby. He was brave today. Dumb, but brave."

"He's a good man, Daddy."

I've told him this a million times. He never believed a word, too blinded by his rage about me growing up.

My mom rubs my back, swaying from side to side as she tries to comfort me and humming a song she used to sing to me every night before bed.

Dad grunts. "I know, baby girl. I know. I have to go now. We're making a plan, and then we're hitting the road. I'm going to bring him home." There's rustling and yelling in the background. "I'll call as soon as we have him."

"Daddy!" I yell before he has a chance to hang up. "I love you."

"Love you too, Gigi. Hey, sugar?" His voice is so sweet and quiet as he asks for my mom.

Mom gives me a sad smile, trying to put on a brave face for me. "Yeah, sweetie. I'm here."

"I love you too," he breathes.

"I love you. Just come home safe, City. Don't be a hero," she tells him. Her face pales as soon as he hangs up, even though she tries to hide it by turning her head.

I drop the phone onto the rug and wrap my body around hers. "Shh," she whispers, cradling me against her chest, rocking me like she used to when I had nightmares. "If anyone can save Pike, your daddy will do it."

If.

She said if anyone can.

No matter how scared I was at the Disciples' compound when DiSantis was after us, at least I was there.

I knew what was happening, but to not know anything is so much more frightening.

"They'll come home to us." She runs her hand down the back of my head in slow, steady strokes. "I know your daddy, baby, and he'll stop at nothing to make you happy."

"I don't want Dad to get hurt either," I whisper, choking back the tears that are lodged in my throat.

My dad's always been my hero. He seems immortal in my eyes, but I know he's like every other man.

He bleeds the same.

Feels the same pain.

Can die just like every other living thing on the planet.

"He'll be fine. They're smart. He has all the guys with him, baby. Don't work yourself into a panic."

Don't work myself into a panic? There isn't any work involved. I am there. My entire body feels the weight of what is happening.

I lie there, letting my mother's gentle rocking dry my tears, but the panic…it still grips me as I think about Pike.

Is Pike hurt?

Is he alone?

Is he afraid?

Are they torturing him?

Is he already dead?

There're so many questions, each one filling me with dread, knotting my stomach into a tighter ball.

"Hello!" Tamara yells out before I hear the front door slam so hard, I'd be shocked if the photos in the foyer are still hanging. "We came as soon as we heard."

I groan, not feeling like company or putting on a fake smile, pretending not to be completely terrified.

"Come on, baby. Let's go talk to Tam," Mom says, lifting me off the floor as she tries to stand. "It's not good to sit in here too long. I know you're already thinking the worst."

I climb to my feet, swiping at my cheeks with the backs of my fingers, spreading the tears around more than wiping them away. Everything around me is fuzzy like I'm dreaming, but I know I'm very much awake. This isn't a nightmare, but my new reality.

Tamara's in the hallway of my mother's house, holding a bottle of Jack Daniel's in one hand and a box of chocolate in the other. "I came prepared," she says, giving me a small smile, using the glass bottle to push her dark brown hair away from her face.

"I'll leave you guys be. I need a moment alone," my mother mumbles, heading in the other direction without even giving Tamara or Austin a hug.

I turn, following Tam's gaze as she gawks at my mother. I wish I could comfort my mom in the same way she just comforted me. I know she's going to cry. I know my mother better than anyone in the world. She consoled me, but she's just as fearful for my father's life.

How could she not be?

He's her everything and has been for decades.

"How bad is it?" Tamara asks as I turn to face her.

"Bad, Tam. Really bad." I shake my head, twisting my lips and blinking to stop myself from crying again.

"Izzy called and told me to get my ass over here because shit went south. I'm not sure what that means, but I grabbed Austin and headed here…" She holds up the Jack, shaking it, but thank God, she doesn't smile. "Want a drink?"

"I want all the drinks," I tell her, stepping toward the kitchen in heavy, slow movements like the weight of the world is on my shoulders.

Austin's on the couch, hunched over, holding his head.

She goes to the cabinet, opens the door, and grabs two glasses as I slide onto the same barstool I'd been sitting on earlier. "What happened?" she asks.

"They were ambushed, and they took Pike." Saying the words still doesn't make it all feel real. My gaze moves to Austin, and he doesn't move, doesn't even blink.

Tamara's eyes widen as she sets down the glasses in front of her and freezes. "No shit. That is bad."

I nod, fighting back the tears. I will not cry again. I always tell Pike to keep calm, and I have to too.

"They're making a plan to rescue him." I choke on the word rescue, but I somehow rebound, getting the last word out.

"They'll get him. Our guys never come home empty-handed," Tamara reminds me.

"Yeah," I mumble, but I'm not even convinced by my answer. "You okay, Austin?"

Austin grunts, not even looking up at us. "I'm fine," he snaps, but we both know he's lying.

"It's okay to be worried," I tell him. "But I know my dad and uncles—they'll stop at nothing to get Pike back." And that's exactly what I'm worried about too. Not only is Pike's life in danger, they're all in danger.

"This is all my father's fault," Austin whispers before climbing to his feet and storming out of the house.

"Leave him," Tamara tells me when I start to move. "He needs time to process everything." She presses the meaty part of her palms into her eyes and blows out a breath. "I'm not sure Jack was right for this situation. I think this is more a tequila type of crisis. You need to be completely shit-faced."

I'd laugh if things weren't so grave. Breakups always called for the hard stuff because who wanted to remember their broken heart? But this is different. I don't want to be passed out when…

"Jack's good," I tell her, grabbing the bottle from her hands, not needing a glass. Her eyes widen as I twist off the top and lift the entire bottle to my lips.

"Maybe you should…"

I glare at her, opening my mouth, letting the amber liquid wash over my tongue and slide down my throat. I wince a little as my throat burns from the mix of hard liquor and vomit.

"Damn, girl. You're not playing," she teases as her eyebrows shoot up, and I keep guzzling mouthful after mouthful.

I pull the bottle away, gasping for air as I wipe my lips with the back of my hand.

She motions for the bottle, because Tamara is never one to be left out of a party, even if it's not a happy occasion.

I narrow my eyes and hold out the bottle to her, knowing damn well she isn't going to take it. "I just puked and didn't rinse my mouth. You really want to share?"

She shakes her head as her lip curls. "Bitch, you should've used a glass. Gross."

I climb off the stool, taking the bottle with me as I walk around the couch and plop down. "I've never felt so helpless, Tam. They don't even know where he is."

She's next to me a moment later, tearing off the plastic wrapping on the cheap box of chocolates I'm sure she picked up at the drugstore. "What happened exactly?"

I tell her the limited details my father shared, leaving nothing out. Her eyebrows move around as if they have a life of their own as she gawks at me like I've just told her the craziest tale.

"Well, Jesus," she mumbles, holding a piece of chocolate near her lips but not taking a bite. "Doesn't he have one of those fancy-ass watches? I mean, why don't they just track him through GPS?"

I gasp, leaping from the couch and immediately regretting all the Jack. My knees wobble as soon as my feet touch the floor, but I catch myself on the armrest before my face has a chance to get up close and personal with the floor. "You're a genius," I tell her, crouched over, waiting for the room to stop spinning. "A goddamn genius."

She shoves the chocolate into her mouth, smiling at me. "I know. I've always known," she replies while chewing.

I glance around, my eyes blurry from the tears that still haven't stopped and dizzy as a motherfucker. "My phone. Oh my God, where's my phone? I have to call my dad and tell him."

Tamara pushes the chocolates to the side, running toward the kitchen. "I'm on it," she snaps as she grabs my phone and starts tapping away at the screen.

"Yeah, baby?" Dad asks before Tamara's made it back to me.

"Daddy, I know how to find Pike." I speak so fast, it comes out like one single long word.

"Tell me," he replies, and for the first time in what feels like hours, I don't feel so useless anymore.

18

PIKE

"JUST KILL HIM," a man orders like he's not talking about taking a man's life.

My life.

The voices are muffled and distant like I'm dreaming, but I know I'm very much alive.

I can't see anything, but I feel *everything*.

The dampness of the blood that's pooled near my hand after they decided a hammer to the pinkie would make me talk.

The cold cement against my cheeks as I lie on my side, gasping for air after they used my stomach to clean their boots, kicking me so many times, I lost count.

"He could be useful," another man replies somewhere behind me.

"We have the key. What more do we fuckin' need?" the asshole who wants to kill me asks.

"I know he means something to the Disciples. Maybe we could…"

"Don't be a dumb fuck," the asshole snaps. "The Disciples aren't going to give us shit. They wanted the key, but it's a good thing this kid's father is such a fuckin' talker."

"Doesn't hurt to have Chev spying either," the dumbass says, and I know exactly who they're talking about.

Chev earned his cut after I left. He wasn't very talkative, but he took orders without question, always delivering what was required. When the Disciples find out they have a rat in their ranks, they're going to kill him in the most painful way possible.

If they find out.

I try to open my eyes, but the swelling is so bad, nothing's clear.

All I have is the darkness for solace. "Just kill me," I groan the plea, my voice barely loud enough for anyone but me to hear.

I'd rather die than be a pawn in their sick game.

"Shut up!" a man yells, before something connects with my jaw, snapping my head backward.

The searing-hot pain quickly follows, slicing through my system from my face to my lungs. I gasp, choking on my own blood, wishing they'd just put me out of my misery already.

"He's heard too much. Seen even more," another man explains, his voice icy and calm. "Drop him in the Everglades. You know the spot."

"Should we kill him here?" Dumbass asks.

"No. He can walk into his watery grave," Asshole replies.

I'm sorry is my silent apology to Gigi, knowing I'll never get to see her beautiful face again. The pain I've endured at the hands of my captors is nothing compared to the agony she'll feel from my death.

I swallow down the metallic taste coating my tongue, fighting through the pain, reveling in my final hours of being alive.

There's so much about my life I'd change if I could, but if living longer means never being with Giovanna Gallo, I wouldn't change a goddamn thing. I'd die today to know her love. I'd willingly end my life early for an ounce of her softness. She is everything I ever wanted and never had until recently.

I may be taking my last breaths, but I don't have any regrets. The men who live on because I'm here, lying on the ground, have families, and they'll do everything in their power to make sure Gigi carries on. She'll marry someday and have babies.

My chest aches, thinking of their tiny faces looking so much like their mother and knowing I won't be their father. It's a selfish thought, but one I can't stop myself from having.

Hands slide over my arm, gripping me roughly. "Up you go, princess. You're about to get your wish."

I groan, finding my footing but still unable to see more than a thin line of light. "Fuck you," I snap, twisting my shoulder as he tries to pull me upright. "Get your damn hands off me."

"He's a live one," the asshole adds. "He would've been a good soldier."

A loud explosion throws me backward, sending my knees and face back against the cement. I groan as the metallic taste of my blood fills my mouth again, and the shooting pain from hitting the concrete ricochets up my legs.

Gunfire and yelling ring through the room, along with the ringing from the explosion echoing in my ears that I can't seem to stop. I collapse, sprawling out on the cool, damp floor, letting the sweet ache of my injuries remind me I'm still very much alive.

But not for much longer.

"Take his ass outside!" someone yells, a voice I know. A voice I've heard a million times. "Get him out of here quick."

The gunfire doesn't stop as heavy bootsteps come near. "Pike, holy fuck," Morris groans. "Jesus Christ."

Yeah. I'm pretty sure I look as shitty as I feel.

"Come on. Let's go," he orders, touching my arm gently like there aren't bullets whizzing near his head.

I lift myself to my knees, wincing as pain shoots up my thighs and causes me to gasp for air. I reach out, finding his hands in the darkness, still unable to see. "Morris," I whisper, thinking I'm imagining he's here.

"Yeah, shithead. Get up, or I'm going to poke you in the eyeball to get your ass moving."

That's Morris. He's such a sadistic fuck. I have no doubt, in this moment, bloodied and busted as I am, he would fucking poke me. He punched me when I was shot; why wouldn't he do the same now?

Even with the pain, I muster a crooked smile. "You came."

"If you don't get your ass moving, we're both going to be dead," he tells me, pulling my entire body weight forward until I find my footing.

I hold on to his arm, letting him be my eyes because no matter how hard I try, I can't see a fucking thing. When the warmth hits my skin, I know we're outside but nowhere near safe.

"The guys," I wheeze.

"They're big boys with even bigger guns." Morris pats my hand. "They'll be okay."

"Leave me and go back." I stop walking, letting my hands fall away from his arm. "Don't save me and risk their lives. Go, Morris. If you ever loved me, go save them," I plead.

"Always a fuckin' problem," Morris groans, placing his meaty hand on my shoulder. "Don't move. Stay here."

"Fucker, go!" I yell, crumpling to the gravel.

Where the hell would I go? I can't see six inches in front of my face, let alone far enough to wander off like some lost kitten.

Morris doesn't say another word, but the sound of gravel crunching under his boots makes it clear he finally listened for once.

I lean back, letting the hard rock bite into my skin as I lie flat, relishing the warmth the stones have soaked up from the sun. I let myself drift because the reality is just too much to take.

"Man, he looks like shit," Bear murmurs from above me, waking me. "I mean, he wasn't anything special to look at before, but now…"

"Fuck you," I mutter and wince.

The gravel crunches near my head, followed by gentle hands touching my battered face. "Call an ambulance."

"No." My answer is immediate and firm. "No cops. No hospitals."

"Put him in the truck. We'll have the doc come to the compound and check him out," Morris commands. "I'll call her now and have her meet us there."

"Can you walk?" Joe asks, his hands moving to my hand, lifting my palm upward. "Fucking hell."

"It's fine." I pull my hand back to my body. "I'm not left-handed."

"I wasn't worried about work, son," he says softly, and I can hear the sincerity in his voice. "Help me carry him."

"No," I groan as I push myself upward with the one hand I have that they didn't smash into pieces. "I can walk on my own."

"This should be fun to watch," Bear teases, always the complete asshole.

"Shut up," Joe snaps. "Come on, Pike. Let's get you out of here, and I'll call Gigi from the truck."

"Gigi," I whisper, thinking about my girl and the level of panic she has to be experiencing. "Call her now."

"No," he tells me, the light shifting back and forth as he moves in front of me. "Truck first, and then you can talk to her. We don't need to be here when the cops show up."

He's a bastard, but he's right. The sound of the blast had to draw someone's attention. No doubt the place will be swarming with police soon.

I reach out, and Joe immediately slides his hand in mine, helping me to my feet.

"James, bring the truck!" he yells as we take a step forward, and I gasp for air.

"My fuckin' ribs," I wheeze. "They're broken."

Joe slides his arm behind my back, and I lean on him, letting him guide me through the darkness. "A lot of you is broken, son. A whole hell of a lot."

"In ya go, kid," Thomas orders, one hand on my arm while Joe keeps me steady.

I climb inside the truck, being given the front seat, and collapse backward, sucking in the little breath my broken ribs will allow.

I'm going to live.

I've never been one to cry, but in this moment, with the men piling into the SUV with me, I could. They put their lives on the line to save mine. No one has ever done that. No one has ever cared enough to do something so profound and selfless.

"Daddy?" Gigi's voice comes through the truck speakers.

"We got him, baby girl. He's okay."

"Pike?"

"I'm here, darlin'," I manage the words, not sounding as completely shitty as I feel.

"Oh my God, baby. I've been so worried. I thought you were…"

"I'm not. I'm okay, love."

I'd say more, but I'm too choked up and moved by everything Gallo.

"He's a little banged up," Joe tells her.

Banged up? That's one way of putting it.

"We'll call you when we get back to the compound, okay, princess?"

"Pike?"

"Yeah?"

"I love you," she says softly, her voice cracking.

"Love you too, darlin'," I tell her, unable to keep the emotion from my voice.

"Talk soon," Joe adds, and then there's silence to match the darkness.

"How does that feel?" the MC's doctor asks as she presses a towel against my eyelid after slicing through the skin. "It'll help reduce the swelling and should make it easier for you to see."

"Feels great," I lie, taking the towel from her hand and holding it against my face.

I feel like one-hundred-percent absolute shit. I've never felt this bad in my entire life, but at least I am alive. That's what I hold on to as she checks me over, patching up my busted parts.

"There's not much I can do for the ribs. They'll heal, but it'll be a few months before you feel normal again. Luckily, your jaw isn't broken, but you should get to a dentist soon to make sure your teeth aren't damaged from the boot you took to the face."

She's blurry, but her shape is clearer with each passing second. I can see the shadow of her body and the bright red of her top.

"The pinkie, I stitched and set. You may need surgery on it if it doesn't heal straight. Keep an eye on it. As for the rest of you, I cleaned any wounds, but they're minimal."

I almost laugh. Minimal?

"He gonna live, Doc?" Morris asks, stalking into the room, scrubbing the back of his neck with his hands.

"He'll live."

Morris exhales, sounding relieved. "Thank fuck."

There are a few clicks before she moves away from me, leaving me on the table.

"Thanks, Doc."

"I'll send you the bill." She pats him on the chest, giving him a bright smile before disappearing out the door.

"This is my fault," Morris admits, stalking across the room and pulling out a chair in front of me. "I fucked up."

I glance down, dropping the cloth next to me so I can see him. "It's my father's fault—and Chev's."

"Chev?" Morris raises an eyebrow, cocking his head to the side.

"He's a rat, Morris. A fuckin' rat." I wince and grab my ribs. "That's how the Vipers knew about the drop."

"I'll take care of him." He nods, and I know what that means. Chev is a dead man walking. "You're one lucky SOB," he says, changing the subject.

I shrug, but I know it's the truth.

"Those men, the girl's family, they weren't leaving without you."

I try to smile, but I grimace, hating everything about today. "They're good people."

"The best," Morris agrees and touches my leg. "I knew you were something special."

"Was that before or after you sucker-punched my shoulder?" I ask him.

He barks out a laugh. "Never going to let me live it down, are ya?"

I shake my head. "Never."

Morris studies me as his laughter dies. "I didn't think I'd see you alive again, Pike. I'm happy I was wrong."

"Me too," I mutter.

"You have a whole room of people who want to see you, and then we'll let you rest. You're staying the night and all heading back tomorrow. Tiny's having your room made up so you're comfortable."

"Thanks," I whisper, taking in a man who's been more of a father to me than mine ever was. When he goes to stand, I know there need to be more words. There may not be another chance. His life, the MC life, isn't known for its longevity. "Morris."

He turns around, his dark eyes gazing at me with intensity. "What's wrong?"

"Thank you for always being there for me. I would've been honored to call you brother."

He smiles. "I would've been happy to call you a son," he replies, knowing exactly what those words mean to me.

I don't say anything else. Morris isn't the type of guy you gush to too much about your feelings. I've never heard him utter the words *I love you* to another man, and I'm not going to force him to say them now.

A minute after he leaves, the four men who came to my rescue walk into the room, their gazes sweeping over my body.

"She patched you up good," Joe says, but he's lying. "You don't look too bad."

Bear winces as his eyes soak me in. "He looks like hell," he argues.

James glares at Bear, slapping him in the chest with the back of his hand. "Now's no time for jokes, asshole."

Bear shrugs. "Wasn't joking. Look at him." He throws out his arm toward me. "If hell had a look, it would be that."

Joe ignores him, stalking toward me and stopping

only a few inches away. I crane my neck back, somehow stopping myself from wincing again.

"You scared the shit out of us," he admits, running his hand through his hair. "I thought I was going to have to tell my little girl you died. I thought I was going to have to live with the guilt that I let you go instead of me."

"I went willingly."

He places his hand on my shoulder, regarding me with something I've rarely seen from him—respect. "It was honorable, Pike. Something any of us—" he shifts his head toward James, Thomas, and Bear "—would do for one another, but you didn't have to give your life for ours."

"I did," I tell him, holding his gaze. "I love your daughter, sir, and I couldn't have looked her in the eye if something had happened to any of you. Her world revolves around her family."

He gives me a pained smile. "We'll always be her family, Pike, but you're her world now."

How does someone respond to something like that? Thank you doesn't seem right. It's too monumental from a man who wanted to see me exit her life as quickly as I appeared not too long ago. I have no words. Nothing that can adequately convey how I feel.

"Izzy's going to have my balls," James tells Thomas, cracking his neck toward the door. "I told her I'd avoid killing someone this trip."

“Never make those kinds of promises, brother. I’ve told you this,” Thomas chastises him, shrugging it off.

They’re still two scary motherfuckers. Family or not, my ass is never crossing them. Never.

“You better get your woman under control,” Bear orders, and just like that, everyone’s forgotten I’m a bloody mess.

19

GIGI

"Your life is like a goddamn soap opera," Tamara quips as we stand in the parking lot of the apartment. "I'm almost jealous."

I turn to her, narrowing my eyes. "You're an asshole. This shit isn't fake, Tamara. Pike could've died."

She frowns, glancing down at her sandals. "I know. I'm sorry," she whispers.

My body's buzzing, and every second that passes, I find it more impossible to stand still. "It's fine. I know you were scared for him too."

She was too. She loves Pike just as much as I do. Not in the same way, but he's grown on her. At first, she wasn't convinced he was a one-woman man. It's not like I have the best track record when it comes to relationships. I probably would've thought the same thing if I were in her shoes.

"They here yet?" Austin asks, coming up behind us, hair a mess because he's just crawled out of bed.

I shake my head, turning back to the street and seeing nothing. "They'll be here any minute. Dad said they were at the light."

"Ever feel like you need an epic adventure?" Tamara asks, earning herself another glare.

"Are you for real?"

She shrugs, giving me a smile. "My life is so boring. Like, if white paint had a life, the shade would be Tamara."

I giggle because the stupidity of her statement is too much for me. "You're…"

"TamTam, I can brighten your world," Austin offers, sliding his arm around her shoulder. "Just give me a shot."

"When you become a badass biker man, give me a call," she teases, elbowing him in the ribs. "Read my shirt, kid. Nothing else needs to be said."

"Tattooed boys are my favorite toys," he says slowly, ogling her chest more than the stark-white lettering. "Gigi can tattoo me tomorrow." He smiles, winking at her. "I got you."

She rolls her eyes and groans. "It's a way of life, Aussie, not a decoration. There's nothing sexier than a man covered in ink, riding a Harley," she sighs. "Am I right?"

"Sure. Yeah," I reply without really listening. I'm too busy staring at the street, waiting for my favorite tattooed boy. "Where are they?"

Austin's strong hand is on my shoulder. "They'll be here. He's fine," he reminds me, something he's been doing for the last twelve hours.

"I know." I twist my hands in front of me, shifting from side to side to keep my sanity in check. "But I won't believe it until I see him with my own eyes."

Suddenly, the roar of dozens of motorcycles fills the air, and we all lift our heads, watching as the motorcade enters the apartment complex.

"Holy fuck!" Tamara yells.

"It's like the president has arrived," Austin jokes over my shoulder.

"Damn," I whisper, seeing James's SUV surrounded by bikes, progressing at a steady pace in the middle. I hold my breath as time seems to move slower than usual.

I've never been a patient person, but standing here now, waiting to see Pike again, feels like torture. The ground rumbles under my feet as the line of bikes stops near the curb.

"Breathe, Gigi!" Austin yells in my ear, reaching forward to hold my hand.

I squeeze his fingers, sucking in a deep breath before I pass out as I release them.

Calm down. He's fine.

I don't remember the last time I was this excited and petrified at the same time. Probably never.

When the black SUV rolls to a stop in front of me, I take a step forward, shaking out my hands and the fear that's been plaguing me.

My dad is the first one out, rounding the SUV, barely making eye contact. "Hey, baby," he whispers. "Now, don't panic."

"Don't panic?" I jerk my head back, widening my eyes. "What's that mean?"

"Oh, dear God," Tamara whispers. "That's never good."

She's always quick with the uplifting comments. *Bitch.*

Dad smiles, touching my cheek gently. "He's fine. He doesn't look great, and I don't want you to freak out."

I shrug off my father's touch and take off toward the SUV. My fingers shake as I grip the handle, flinging the door open. The flinch is immediate. The gasp is next.

"Fuck," I hiss, tears filling my eyes at the horror of his battered face and the happiness of him making it home.

"Missed you too, darlin'," he drawls, turning slowly to swing his jeans-covered legs out of the truck.

I want to rush forward, pepper his face with kisses, but I can't seem to move. It's like I'm frozen to the ground, the reality of what happened written all over his face.

"Baby," I whisper, my voice cracking as I cover my mouth.

"You said I was pretty, Joe. She doesn't seem too impressed with my makeover," Pike laughs as his boots touch the ground.

"I tried to prepare her." Dad shrugs.

"Didn't work," Pike tells him, grimacing as he straightens and starts to take a step.

I move forward, reaching for him. "Can I touch you?" I ask.

He nods, giving me a smile. "I'm not going to break."

"It looks like you're already broken, yo," Tamara, the comedian, taunts.

"Ignore her," I groan, but Pike's smile never falters.

"I am, but I've never been happier to be alive," Pike confesses, holding me close with one arm.

"We're going to go," Dad says, watching as I help Pike up on to the sidewalk.

"What about them?" Austin ticks his chin toward the bikers.

"They'll be nearby for the night."

I lift my gaze, finding Morris planted on the front bike, watching us. I smile at him, happy as hell he's here. He immediately sends a wink back my way.

Pike turns, taking me with him. "Joe?"

"Yeah?"

"Thank you," Pike says simply.

My dad looks at me and then toward Pike. "No thank-yous are needed for family, kid."

I gape at him, wondering what in the hell happened to change his attitude. I get Pike almost died, but it sure as hell wasn't the first time. Dad wasn't all kumbaya after the shootout at the Disciples' compound. Granted, Pike didn't look like absolute shit then either.

"That was some crazy shit right there," Tamara says, blinking at my father like she thinks she must've been hearing things too.

"We went through a lot," Pike tells us. "More shit than I'll ever tell you."

I grab a better hold of his belt loop, careful not to put too much pressure on his ribs. "I want to know everything."

He shakes his head. "Some things are better left unsaid, darlin'."

"Our place or hers?" Austin asks, walking slowly at his brother's other side.

Pike glances over, smiling at his little brother. "Ours. I want my bed and my girl tonight."

Amen.

I tuck my hand under my cheek, trying to hold back the tears. "I was so scared, baby. So, so scared."

"Come here," he breathes, motioning for me to scoot closer.

"I don't want to hurt you."

"You won't."

I move an inch closer, but still far enough away I don't cause his side of the bed to move.

"Darlin', I need you against me." He smiles.

"You're all…" I motion to his bare chest with my hand, wincing.

"I know, but you can't hurt me any more than I already am. Just come here and stop being so stubborn."

I snort, pushing myself up on my elbow. "I'm not stubborn."

He reaches up, brushing my hair away from my face with his fingers. "I thought I'd never see you again." His eyes search my face, and I do my best not to cry, but fail. "Don't cry again," he pleads.

"I'm a mess," I groan, wiping my cheek on my shoulder. "I'm sorry."

I've cried more tears today than yesterday. Every time I looked at him, a fresh wave would overtake me. His swollen eyes and bruised jaw are a constant reminder of everything he went through.

He slides his fingers across my cheek until they're in my hair, my face resting in his palm. "Don't ever be sorry."

My lips find his wrist, one of the only places on him that isn't busted. "I just love you so much."

"Come here," he orders again, digging his fingers into my neck. "I want to hold you."

I don't argue this time, needing the skin-on-skin contact as much as he does. I press my chest against his side, the one without the broken ribs, and place my head on his shoulder.

"We need to talk," he says with so much seriousness, I gaze upward into his green eyes, quickly sobering.

"What's wrong? Am I hurting you?" I start to move, but he holds me down with his hand on my shoulder.

"No, you're not hurting me."

"Then what?"

"When I was lying there, sure I was a dead man, I did a lot of thinking."

"Yeah?"

Oh my God. Is this the moment? The one every girl

dreams about? The one I'll tell my children about someday?

"If I were to die…" he starts.

So wrong, Gigi. So fucking wrong.

"Stop," I whisper and push myself upward and away from him. "I don't want to hear anymore."

"If I were to die…" he repeats.

I shake my head and close my eyes. "It's not happening."

"Darlin', listen." His touch is whisper-soft but unmistakable. "I need to say this."

I take a deep breath and open my eyes again, knowing it's only fair to let him say whatever's on his mind. He almost died, for shit's sake, and no matter how badly I don't want to hear what's about to come next, I have to let him say it. "I'm listening."

"I don't plan on going anywhere anytime soon, but I need to know that if something happens to me, you'll keep on going. You'll find a husband, make babies, grow old, and be happy."

I twist my lips, blinking at him. "Are you for real right now?"

He nods.

"If I were to die, would you ever be happy?" I question him.

"Well, no," he confesses without batting a fucking eyelash.

"Neither would I. So, can we talk about something else?"

"Only if you lie down again."

"As long as you don't talk about dying anymore." I place my hand on my chest, trying to calm myself down. "My heart can't take it."

He nods, grabbing my arm and pulling me toward him. "It's the last thing I want. I don't think I can ever have enough time with you."

I curl into him and press my lips to his shoulder. "I know this is a strange thing to say, but I feel like I've known you my entire life."

"I don't want to remember what life was like before you." He runs his fingers through my hair, and I can't hold back the moan. "I wasn't livin' until you came into my world, darlin'. I was existing. There's a difference."

"I can't imagine my life without you, Pike."

"I love you," he whispers.

I gaze up and smile. "I love you too."

We lie there in silence, lightly touching each other.

If I didn't know better, I'd swear I was dreaming.

20

GIGI

Two months later...

I turn in my seat, Pike's warm hand resting on my knee, to glare at Austin in the back seat of my pickup. "If you say a word to our parents about our first stop, you're not going to make it to your eighteenth birthday."

Austin swallows, his Adam's apple bobbing. "Come on, ladies," he says, sliding his arms behind Lily and Tamara. "Would I do something like that?"

"Yes," all three of us answer in unison.

Lily elbows him in the ribs. "We may not kill you, but I'll hold you down and let Tamara pull your fingernails out."

Austin pales, and I bite my lip to stop myself from giggling. Lily's hard-core and gives zero fucks. I adore the bitch so much and wish she'd gone to college near us instead of venturing out on her own. Fuckin' scholarships.

"You wouldn't do that." Austin's voice cracks, but he keeps on rolling. "You love me."

Tamara runs her palm across his hand. "That's why we'd only do your fingernails and leave you alive, Aussie. We'd never kill you, but we're not above torturing you." She smiles, and it's so beautifully wicked, my heart grows three sizes like the Grinch at the end of my favorite Christmas movie.

"You bitches are vicious," Austin groans, pulling his hand back and tucking his fingers between his legs. "So fucking vicious. I won't say a word. Jesus, give me some credit. I memorized the story, practicing it and spitting it back perfectly when they questioned me at the shop."

It's not like they can tell us no. We are all adults after all, living on our own. And even though our families are nosy, they don't have the right to tell us what to do.

But that doesn't mean any of us want to hear their shit either. God, if my dad found out we were stopping by the compound for a night, I'd get a freaking earful until I went deaf. He'd probably still keep yelling, figuring his deep, husky voice would penetrate somehow.

Lily winks at me, knowing just like I do, there's no harm in scaring the piss out of the guy. We've learned one thing in our two decades together—we never snitch on each other.

"Loosen up, Aussie. This is going to be a fun weekend." Tamara reaches up and pinches Austin's cheeks, trying to get him to relax.

He shakes his head, digging his fingers deeper. "I just wanted to see some T&A. Someday, you'll trust me."

Lily drags her finger down his other cheek, smiling when he starts to squirm. "You're going to see some T&L, and that's about it, li'l guy."

"T&L?" Austin asks.

"Tamara and Lily," Lily laughs.

Austin rolls his eyes. "You two are like my sisters." He pretends to gag, but I know he's lying. The horndog hasn't let up, and even though he's nervous as fuck between the two of them right this second, he's loving the attention they're giving him.

"Here's the rules," Pike tells us, glancing in the rearview mirror and squeezing my leg. "This is for everybody and not just Austin, ya hear?"

"Yes!" the four of us groan, knowing Big Daddy Pike is about to lay down the law and it's going to be boring as fuck.

"I lived with these people. I know their ways. This is one of the tamest parties of the year. The kids will be there, but that doesn't mean there isn't bad shit happening if you go looking for it."

"Oh yeah?" Lily asks, scooting forward. "What kind of shit?"

"You won't go lookin' for it, so don't worry about it, Lily," he tells her before bringing his eyes back to the road.

"Drugs?" Austin asks with a little too much enthusiasm.

Pike's steely gaze slices to the mirror. "If you go within so much as five feet of drugs, I'm cutting your dick off and shoving it down your throat."

I wince, imagining the horror and pain. Pike can say what he wants, but I know he'd never lay a finger on his brother…drugs or not.

"You're just as bad as Gran," Austin mutters.

"That goes for all of you. No drugs. No hard liquor. I don't want to be dragging your sloppy asses out of some asshole's room or rescuing you from a crazy gang bang that sounded like fun because you were too drunk to realize they weren't talking about pounding rocks."

"What?" I ask, glancing at him, so fucking confused.

He shrugs but keeps on rolling. "Don't embarrass me, and for the love of God, don't embarrass yourself."

"You have a way with words, Shakespeare," Lily teases, covering her mouth immediately to snicker into the palm of her hand.

"Sure thing, Joe. Whatever you say," Tamara adds because she's a shithead and loves pissing off Pike.

Pike wrinkles his forehead. "What did you call me?"

I place my hand on his forearm, somehow managing not to laugh. "We hear you, boss man. Calm down a little. It's Labor Day weekend, and we're supposed to have fun."

"Fun," he mutters, glancing toward the top of the truck cab. "I don't care about fun, Gigi. I didn't even want to go to this damn party, but you just had to jump at Morris's offer."

I bristle at his choice of words, tightening my grip on his arm. "These people were your people once, Pike. They saved your life twice," I remind him. "Relax a little. We had fun the last time we were here. Remember?"

He turns his head so slowly, eyes so icy, the hairs on the back of my neck stand up, looking for a quick exit. "Last time we were here—" he points toward the compound "—we almost died."

I nod, remembering it well and still happy as shit we lived. "But we didn't." I put a smile on my face, hoping to make him chill out. "We were whisked away without even being able to say thank you to the men who put their lives on the line to save us. I think we could at least have a beer with them and let them know their bravery didn't go unappreciated."

He groans. "You know I love these guys. They were my family for years, but damn, Gigi. They're not the fun-loving bunch you think they are. They're one-percenters."

"Damn," Lily squeaks, "they're that rich?"

"You seriously need to get out more," Tamara tells Lily, leaning over Austin, giving her a *you're a freaking idiot* stare.

All I can do is roll my eyes, ignoring the cute, clueless bitch in the backseat. She's such a brainiac; she knows her chemistry way better than her MC lingo. Poor, poor Lily.

"What?" Lily asks, glancing around the truck like we're supposed to clue her in, but I don't have time for all that.

"Don't worry, babe," Austin tells her, finally removing his hands from his legs to tap her hand. "I got you."

"Now," Pike barks, turning around, facing the three goofballs in the backseat. "Am I going to have to go into Gallo witness protection after this trip because one of you assholes has to act like a tool?"

Three headshakes are immediate, and then he brings his eyes to me. "You going to behave too?"

I smile and shrug. "Don't I always?"

Pike blinks, but the corner of his lip twitches, and I know I have him.

I lean back in the chair, comfortably sandwiched between Pike's thighs, gazing up at the sky. "I take back what I said before."

"What?"

"About this place being like Disney World for crack whores and criminals." I laugh, resting my head on his shoulder as he strokes the bare skin of my shoulder with his fingers.

"What do you think now?" he asks in a husky voice, and my skin tingles with each pass of his fingers.

"This—" I lift my hand, pointing toward the bounce houses and all the other family shit all over the compound's yard "—is totally the Disney World for them bitches. Before was more like Chuck E. Cheese."

My body shakes as Pike laughs, the deep, rich sound sending shivers down my spine. "Darlin', you're beyond fucked up."

"But you love me?" I ask, turning my face to look up into his beautiful green eyes.

He nods without hesitation. "More than breathing," he tells me, and my stomach flutters.

I snuggle into him as he drops his hand, sliding his arms around me. "Are you relaxed yet?" I ask, watching as the club whores prance around, showing their goods to whoever will look. "You were wound pretty tight before."

His lips brush the skin near my ear, and I close my eyes, getting lost in his touch. "I'm just scared," he admits, and my eyes snap open.

Pike rarely says those words. He hasn't uttered them since the last time we were here.

"There's nothing to be scared about."

He tightens his hold, his warm breath skidding across my neck. "Any time we're here, we're a target. They're an MC, Gigi. This isn't a hobby. Bad shit happens all the time." He exhales, pulling me with him as he leans back into the chair. "There wasn't a day when I lived here that something crazy didn't happen. And just being here with you guys has me on edge. I won't relax until we're at least thirty miles away from the gates."

"We can go now," I offer.

"We'll stay. It's dark, late, and I'm tired as fuck. We'll crash here tonight, but we're gone first thing in the morning."

"I asked for an early check-in in Daytona."

"Good, darlin'. I could use a little downtime. We've been going nonstop for what feels like an eternity."

"Pike?"

"Yeah."

"I'm about to sweat my face off, so do you mind if

I have a beer since we're all about relaxing now?" I smile into the darkness.

"Beer's fine, but not tequila," he teases with a hint of laughter.

I push myself up, leaving the safety of his arms, and roll my eyes as soon as I turn around to face him. "Don't forget, without the tequila, we wouldn't be where we are now."

He's out of his seat, hands on my hips, before I have a chance to react. A slow, small smile crosses his lips. "Darlin', you were mine the moment I laid eyes on you. Tequila or no tequila, we'd still be right where we are now."

I gulp, taking in those endlessly deep eyes. "Yeah," I whisper, knowing what he's saying is true.

"Yeah," he tells me, gripping my hips rougher. "I wasn't letting you walk out of that bar without me."

"You're really cocky."

One corner of his mouth moves higher. "I got my girl, didn't I?"

"Mr. Cuervo got you this girl," I tease.

Pike slides his hands to my ass, pulling my body against his cock. "Keep lyin' to yourself, beautiful."

"Pike!" Austin's voice comes from behind me.

Pike lifts his head immediately, eyes searching through the crowd to find his brother.

"Over here," the same pain-in-the-ass teenager says again.

Pike dips his face, bringing his lips so close to mine, I can't breathe without taking him in. "Promise me we won't have kids for a few years. I don't like dividing my time."

My belly flops again because, holy freaking hell, he's talking about babies. "I promise." I nod.

"Pike!"

"Jesus Christ," Pike growls, turning me around and tucking me under his arm, resting his hand on my shoulder. "Let's go see what he wants."

"Dude." Austin runs his hand through his hair, eyes wide and panicked. "I can't find Tamara. She was here one minute, talking to some guys, and then…"

Oh. Freaking. Hell. Pike's body stiffens, and my eyes widen. "I will fuckin' kill…"

"Baby," I beg, grabbing his hand before he has a chance to curl his fingers into a fist. "Tam's a smart girl. I'm sure she's just using the bathroom or something."

I'm lying.

I know that little badass-biker-seeking whore is off sucking face with some guy who, no doubt, has a death wish.

Heaven help us all.

21

PIKE

"WHERE THE HELL IS TAMARA?"

Lily's eyes widen as soon as she turns around to look at me. "Um…" She looks everywhere but at me, twisting her hands in front of her body. "Around," she lies.

Gigi's hand tightens around my bicep. "Calm down, baby. She's just having fun."

"Fun?" I snap, sucking in a breath as I turn my face up to the sky, growling like a wild animal.

"People are looking at us," Gigi whispers.

"I don't give a shit who's looking," I tell her, bringing my gaze back to her face.

"Lily." Austin steps between Lily and me. "Which way did she go?"

Lily points toward the clubhouse and stands on

her tiptoes, casting her gaze over Austin's shoulder. "Just don't freak out on her, Pike."

I run my hand through my hair, concentrating on my breathing because I'm already freaking out. I'm responsible for these women. It doesn't matter how old they are; they're still here with me. I can't go back to Tamara's father and say "She's a grown woman" if shit goes bad. They're going to blame me and only me for anything and everything.

"She alone?" I ask, somehow managing to speak without sounding like I'm ready to murder someone.

Lily's fingers twist around a few strands of her hair as she eyes me. "No," she squeaks, "but she's safe."

I bite out a bitter laugh.

Safe? There's not a man in this compound I'd call safe for a girl like Tamara Gallo. I don't care how wild she is; there's a difference between college boys and biker badasses. She's never waded into this territory, and no matter how sweet a brother can be, he's always after the same thing.

"Maybe Lily and I should go find her," Gigi offers when I don't give a reply. "It'll only take us a few minutes."

"No." My response is immediate. "I'm going in there, and the three of you—" I sweep my gaze around to them "—will stay here and not move."

"I'll keep an eye on them," Austin promises, trying to be the man.

He has a good heart. My parents didn't fuck him up, thank god. And when he actually becomes a man, he's going to be the best one in the family. But for now, he's still a kid.

"Doofus, you're, like, ten." Lily rolls her eyes at Austin.

Gigi's hand is on my arm again, holding on tight. "We won't move, baby. But promise me something."

"What?" I growl, unable to unclench my jaw.

"Don't kill her. Don't start a war about whatever's going on in there." She throws out her hand toward the building. "She's just being Tamara, and she's an adult."

I grit my teeth, trying to give my girl a smile but failing miserably. "It's not her you have to be worried about."

"Well, shit," Austin drawls, running his hand through his hair, spinning in a circle like he knows what's about to happen. "Want help?"

I shake my head, leaning forward and placing my fingers under Gigi's chin, bringing her large, scared eyes to me. "I won't start a war and I'd never hurt Tamara, but whatever asshole she's with is fair game."

"Shit," Lily mutters, inching toward the car and away from our small group. "Maybe we should wait by the car in case we need a quick escape."

Something about her words breaks through my anger, and I laugh, shaking my head. "We're not going anywhere, Lily. Relax. I'm just going to go in there and bring Tamara out. She shouldn't be inside with anyone, especially not someone from the club."

"He looked really nice," Lily adds, giving me a big, fake smile. "Like, really sweet and a great guy."

Somehow, I don't roll my eyes at the naïveté in her statement. Ted Bundy looked nice too, and that didn't turn out well at all for any of his victims.

Gigi glares at her cousin. "Shut up, Lily. You're not helping anything," she tells her before tipping her head back to glance up at me. "Go. We'll wait here, but keep calm, baby. Calm."

I kiss her quickly and leave, knowing the three of them are staring at my back as I walk toward the clubhouse. I remind myself of Gigi's words in her sweet voice.

Keep calm.

"Where ya headed, brother?" Morris asks when I'm within a few feet of the door and am reaching for the handle.

I swing my head around, not moving the rest of my body. "I'm lookin' for someone."

Morris raises an eyebrow, waiting for me to explain.

"Gigi's cousin is in there with one of the brothers."

Morris nods and laughs. "Just don't start something unless your ass is ready to finish it."

I stare at him with a straight face. "I never start anything I can't finish. You know this."

He studies me for a second, the laughter still on his lips. "I know, Pike. But remember, she ain't your kid either." He opens the door and steps inside, holding it open for me and ticking his head to the side.

My eyes follow his movement, and my body stiffens. Tamara's at the bar, sitting in the lap of some guy I don't know, his hands a little too close to her ass for my liking.

She tips her head back and laughs loudly. "You are just too much, Crow."

"Yeah, doll?" he asks her, eyes sweeping down her neck and straight to her tits.

The clubhouse is virtually empty. Everyone's outside waiting for fireworks except for a few stragglers milling around the public space near the bar. Crow and Tamara are the only two sitting down, looking like they're having a great time.

I let out a shaky breath, happy as fuck I didn't catch him balls deep inside her. I would've had to pound his face in and probably get my ass kicked in return by a few brothers too.

"Pike!" Tamara screeches as soon as she sees me,

waving her hands high in the air like she's excited to see me. "Come meet my new friend."

Fucking women.

Crow cranes his neck, glancing at me over his shoulder, hands tightening around Tamara. "Ah. The man. The myth. The legend," he mutters, his eyes raking over my body like he's sizing me up, waiting for me to strike.

There're two ways I can handle this—I could march over, drag Tamara off his lap, and yank her ass outside, dealing with Crow afterward, or I could try to be civil and coax her outside without making a huge scene and getting Gigi mad at me.

I stalk forward, hands clenched, shoulders tight. "It's just Pike."

Tamara lifts her leg, kicking out the stool next to her and Crow. "Come talk with us," she says, and she's in such a cute and playful mood, I hate that I'm going to rain all over her happy parade.

I slide onto the stool, resting my elbow on the bar, eyeing the guy who's now her ass cushion. "You look familiar, Crow."

He gives me a toothy grin, the white of his teeth a stark contrast to the black in his beard. "We've met a time or two," he mutters casually before glancing back at the girl in his lap.

I narrow my gaze, locking in on his hands and the ink covering them. The solid black wings with the tips grazing the top of each finger. "Weren't you out of New York?"

He nods but doesn't bother looking at me. "After all the shit went down, I took Tiny up on his offer to join the Disciples. So far—" he slides his hand up higher on Tamara's waist, fingertips way too close to her breasts "—it's been fucking perfection."

I'd met Crow a handful of times, and he seemed like an all right guy. Different from the others, even. Quiet like me. Reserved yet not, when the time was right. But he is still a biker. Still wrong for Tamara, no matter how nice he makes himself sound.

She blinks at him like she's drunk on his gaze. "It's worked out great for me, handsome." Tamara winks at him, sliding her arm around his neck like they've been friends forever.

"Gigi's looking for you," I blurt out, and Tamara's head snaps back.

"Well, shit," she mutters, never missing a beat. "Tell my girl to come in here."

I lift an eyebrow. "I think you should go see her," I emphasize the word go, but she just blinks at me like I'm speaking another language.

"Don't be a party pooper, Pike. I'm having so much fun, and Crow's legs are…" She trails off, blushing as he winks at her. "So comfortable."

"Doll," Crow says softly, almost sweetly. "Give us men a few minutes to talk. Go grab that cousin of yours, and the four of us can have a drink and hang out, yeah?"

Tamara's eyes widen as the smile on her face grows. "Baby," she croons, and I almost vomit. "I'll do whatever you want."

I cough, barely holding my shit together. *I will not kill him. I will not kill him.* I repeat the words to myself in a slow, steady rhythm so I don't lunge toward him, doing something Gigi will make me regret.

Tamara climbs off his lap, running her fingers through his beard as her feet find the floor. "Promise me you won't go anywhere."

He glances down at his lap. "I'm not moving a muscle, sweetheart. My thighs are going to miss your sweet ass. So, do me a favor and make it quick."

Tamara doesn't even blink or seem to care that he just bossed her around because he twisted it up in a nice way. She nods, not even hesitating as she takes off toward the door.

"What?" I growl with my jaw clenched so fucking tight, my teeth ache.

Crow tilts his head to the side, a smirk playing behind his beard. "Calm your shit, brother. We're just flirting. I know that girl," he says, motioning toward the door with his chin, "is not a club whore. She's sweet. A little naïve, but still sweet."

"First, I'm not your brother." I glare at him because so help me God, I want to murder him. "Second, she's very naïve. Third, she is sweet, but you'll never know how sweet as long as I'm breathing."

He stands up, reaches over the bar, grabbing a few beer bottles that are sitting there. "Relax," he tells me, offering me a beer. "I know where to dip my wick, and it isn't in her."

I take the beer, eyeing him as I twist off the top, throwing it onto the bar. "She's my family, Crow. I won't let you or any of the other guys here near her without a fight."

He leans his head back, drinking half the bottle down his throat before he speaks again. "I'm still finding a place here with the Disciples. I'm the new meat, and from what I've seen so far, I'm not impressed by the buffet."

"Why Tamara?" I ask point-blank.

"She's sweet and pure. Ever have something so perfect, you want to do whatever you can to hold on to it?"

"Every fucking day," I admit.

"I ain't looking to cause problems. I found her in here an hour ago talking to Lefty, and I did whatever I had to do to get her away from him."

My stomach drops at the mention of Lefty's name. The scariest and fucking nuttiest bastard in the club. Lefty has more kills to his name than anyone else, and he doesn't always think clearly, too fucked up on coke most of the time.

"I did you a solid by talking to that girl. Didn't know I was doing me a solid too." He smiles, going back to his beer and turning his face away from me.

"Fuck," I groan, knowing I could've walked in on something so much worse than Tamara in Crow's lap.

"Yep," he barks. "I think you owe me a thank-you."

"Never fuckin' happenin'," I snarl, even though I should say thank you to him for rescuing her from a madman.

Crow laughs, fisting his hand before punching me in the shoulder like we're long-lost friends. "Just let me flirt with the pretty thing. I'm harmless, and tomorrow, I'll be nothing but a memory. I could use a little good in my life, even if it's only for a few hours."

I inhale, tightening my hands around my beer bottle, about to tell him to fuck off when Gigi, Tamara, Lily, and Austin walk through the door, sounding more like twenty people with all their chatter than four.

"This is Crow," Tamara tells Gigi, looking at him like he walks on water, fluttering her pretty black eyelashes his way. "He's my guy."

I almost choke on my beer, pounding on my chest as Gigi gives me the side-eye.

"Gigi," Gigi says, holding out her hand to him, elbowing me because I can't stop coughing on the goddamn beer.

"I see pretty and sweet runs in the family," Crow flirts, lifting Gigi's hand up to his lips like I'm not fucking sitting there.

"Watch it," I bite out, finally clearing the beer from my throat.

He drops Gigi's hand, glancing over at Lily. "And who's this beautiful creature?"

Lily blushes immediately, lifting her shoulders with wide eyes like she's a baby lamb headed to slaughter. "I'm Lily," she chirps, all bashful and nothing like her cousins.

Tamara climbs back into Crow's lap, staking her territory before he can say anything more or reach out to touch Lily in any way. "I missed you," she whispers, reaching up to touch his beard with her long, thin fingers.

His eyes twinkle as he looks at her. "Missed you too, dollface."

"Oh, good lord," Gigi whispers. My hand goes to her waist, pulling her against me as she gawks at them.

"Hey," Austin adds like the forgotten one of the group because he's a dude and doesn't have the right parts to get noticed around here. "I'm this one's brother." He tips his head in my direction.

Crow's eyebrows shoot up. "For-real brother?"

"For real." Austin smiles, looking genuinely proud

of being related to me for the first time ever. "At least that's what my birth certificate says."

I know one thing in this moment. I will never tell him we don't share the same father. It's nothing he needs to know. I'm all he has left in this world, and I don't want to fill his head with any doubts or questions. I went most of my life thinking that cold bastard Colton Moore was my daddy, and telling the world the opposite wouldn't change a goddamn thing after all the hell he put me through.

"I can see it," Crow says, turning his attention back to the girl in his lap.

"This isn't good," Gigi whispers as she tucks her face into my neck, trying not to be heard by her cousin.

"We talked. He knows how to behave."

"I'm more worried about how Tam's going to behave."

I laugh, running my fingers up her arm. "We just won't let her out of our sight, darlin'."

"Great," Gigi grumbles with a frown as she looks up at me. "I've turned into my mother."

22

GIGI

We headed to the beach while the guys stayed behind, crashing in the beds as soon as our rooms were ready. This is just what I needed after a sleepless night at the compound, watching over Tamara and Crow like I was my parents.

Ugh.

"Who are you talking to?" I ask Tamara, glancing over as she feverishly pecks away at her phone screen.

She hasn't put the damn thing down since we left the compound. She's taken her phone everywhere, even to the bathroom, and is giddy every time the damn thing vibrates.

"Crow." She smirks, giving me the side-eye. "He's just too much fun."

I know the allure of a bad boy. Pike sucked me in from the moment I met him. Damn it. I always told myself I'd never fall in love with someone like my father.

And what happened?

Boom. Joe Junior fell right into my lap.

Not really. I fell into his bed, planting my ass there for a solid week because he was just too good to walk away from.

And now… Now, I can't imagine life without him.

"Fun's one word for him," Lily grumbles on my other side, stretching out her body on her towel. "I'm so fucking tired because of you two assholes."

"We didn't need babysitters," Tamara spits back, not bothering to look in Lily's direction. "We're both grown adults."

Instead of cuddling up in Pike's old room like we did last time, he and I stayed on the couches in the common area with Tamara, Crow, Lily, and Austin. I tried my best not to think about all the shit that went down on those couches before I sat on them.

"Ha," Lily snaps. "I swear you're just trying to do whatever you can to make everyone around you crazy-worried and stressed as shit."

Tamara rolls her eyes, dropping her hand near her hips. "I'm just trying to have some fun. We're only young once. I mean, look at our parents. It's all bills, crying kids, and the same old bullshit every day. This is our one chance to live life and be free before adulthood sucks the life out of us."

"There's a difference between living and having a death wish," Lily tells her, scooting her ass down on the towel to block her face with the nearby umbrella.

"Tam has a point." I can't believe I'm agreeing with Tamara about this, but I keep going and try not to put too much thought into it. "I'm done with college, and you two will be after next year. We're going to be old before we know it."

Lily sighs. "I wish we could go back to high school and do it all over again."

"Fuck no," I spit out, thinking about the heartaches and bullshit we all went through during those four years. "Maybe back to freshman year of college, but there's no way I'd go back to high school."

"Ugh," Tamara mutters, wiggling her toes as her silver glitter polish twinkles in the sun. "I hated those years."

Lily sits up, resting her upper body on her elbows. "They weren't so bad."

Tamara and I both turn our heads, gawking at our cousin because she must have amnesia if she thinks those were golden years we'd ever want to relive.

"It sucked ass, Lil. Are you ill right now?" Tamara laughs.

Lily shakes her head. "Life was simple then. What was our biggest headache? Homework. I mean, come on. No job. No responsibilities."

"Curfew. Parents. Rules. What about that sounds like fun?" I ask.

Lily lifts a shoulder, staring out across the rolling waves. "Time just moves so fast, and for the first time ever, we're all going to be in different places."

My heart aches for a moment because she's right. When Tamara and I were at FSU, Lily would come up on weekends and breaks, and we'd party our asses off. But now… Now, I'll be home, and they'll be far, far away from me.

"In a year, you'll both be home, though, right?" I ask, looking between my two sisters from other misters.

I can't imagine going very long without seeing them. They are as much a fixture in my life as my two little sisters. We grew up together. Got into trouble together. Started dating around the same time, totally not telling our parents about that either. We know one another's secrets, and there aren't two other girls on the planet I am closer to than them.

Lily sighs and Tamara shrugs.

I sit up quickly, spinning around on my ass and clutching the towel between my hands. "What the hell? You two have to come back. You can't leave me."

"You have Pike now," Tamara admits like he's a replacement.

I blink. "Tam, be serious now. He can never replace you."

Lily brushes her hand against mine before linking our fingers together. "I'm trying to get into USF to work on my doctorate and I hope to do my residency at a hospital in Tampa, but you never know, Gigi."

I can feel my eyes starting to water as my nose tickles. "You have to come home."

"We're trying, babe. We're trying," Tamara says, lifting her phone back up to her face as soon as it vibrates. "Jesus Christ," she gasps, eyes going wide as saucers.

"What?" I smack her legs, trying to look at her screen, but she turns her phone the other way.

"When is it too early in a relationship for a dick pic?" she asks, keeping her eyes trained on the screen with a smirk.

I wince, knowing there isn't a cock in the world that looks good in a selfie. "It's always too early," I tell her, shaking my head and totally judging the super-dreamy—her words, not mine—Crow. "Pike's never sent me one."

Lily lunges over me, ripping Tamara's phone from her hands and stares at the screen. "You fuckin' liar. It's just words." Lily tosses the phone back toward Tamara. "Boring."

"I just wanted to see what you'd do. You guys ever

ask for a dick pic?" Tamara raises an eyebrow, staring at us.

I shake my head. "Why the fuck would I want a dick pic?"

"You're such a weirdo," Lily scoffs, scrunching up her nose at Tamara. "I don't know how we're related."

"If you weren't dating Pike," Tamara teases, looking right at me, "I'd say Mallory was right about you. But he gives you some points in the cool column."

What? Mallory was the biggest asshole, and if it weren't for her sister Mary, we wouldn't have been friends. Tamara knows this. She hated Mallory just as much as I did.

I cross my arms, twisting my lips and glaring at my cousin. "I'm cool, and Mallory's a tool."

I mean, I am. I've never been the nerdy type. I'm not too uptight to party. I could hang out with just about anyone and have a good time. I'm not afraid to get drunk and let loose. Hell, I slept with Pike, and I didn't even know the man. Maybe not my best moment and it could've ended much differently, but I wouldn't change a goddamn thing in my life.

She shakes her head. "So not, but you think you are. And you." Tamara tilts her head, studying Lily. "You used to be pretty badass, but now your nose is always stuck in a book, worried about that perfect GPA."

Lily smiles, running her fingers down her legs like she's trying to calm herself. "The world couldn't handle three Tamaras."

"Someday, you're going to bust free, Lil, and I'm going to be there cheering you on."

"I don't have time to bust free," Lily sighs, falling backward on the blanket and spreading out her body. "I'm so exhausted."

"Maybe we need to go on an epic adventure." Tamara taps her chin. When she starts thinking up crazy shit, I know we're in trouble. "Gigi can't come because she has to work, but you and I could totally do it."

I grind my teeth, hating that somehow, I'm the adult in the group. "I hate you two."

"No, you don't." Tamara smiles. "Plus, if I had a hottie like that in my bed, I wouldn't be going anywhere except to pick up more birth control."

I roll my eyes. "Adulting sucks."

"I can't go on an epic adventure," Lily sighs. "Maybe next summer."

"Maybe Crow will be my adventure," Tamara comments, not looking at us when she speaks.

"Don't," I warn her. "Don't get into something you'll regret."

"Do you regret meeting Pike?" she throws back, lifting one perfectly plucked eyebrow.

"Of course I don't."

"He's no different from Crow."

I blink at her. "Yes, he is."

She leans back, placing a rolled-up towel under her head, looking cool as a cucumber. "How?"

"They just are," I tell her, lying back too, ready to pass out.

"They're both badass biker dudes. They're both Disciples."

"Pike was never a Disciple."

"Semantics," she says. "They both ride Harleys."

"You're talking nonsense." I wave her off with my hand. "Pike is more than a biker."

"So's Crow."

"Do you literally want your father to shit a brick?" I ask her point-blank.

Tamara laughs. "Anthony will survive."

"I'll remind him of that when you're off on your epic badass biker adventure."

There's a shadow suddenly covering us before we hear, "Who needs sunscreen?" coming from Austin's mouth.

I tip my head back, seeing the horny teenager almost drooling from all the skin. You'd think we were naked with the way his eyes are almost popping out of his skull. Our bikinis are modest compared to some of the others on the beach. It's not like our tits are completely hanging out, even if he is acting like it.

"Close your mouth, Austin," Tamara tells him, pulling her sunglasses back down over her eyes. "Coffee." She lifts her hand, snapping her fingers.

"As you wish, my queen," he says, falling to his knees at her side.

I grumble at how completely annoying Tamara and Austin are.

"Babe, come in the water with me," Pike orders, walking up behind Austin, carrying a cardboard carton filled with coffees.

"Coffee first," I groan, lifting a hand, being overdramatic.

Fuck. I feel like a tractor ran over me, leaving me for dead. I used to be able to stay up all night, party my ass off, and pop out of bed for class. But now it's all roadkill city.

Pike sits down above my head, pushing one of the cups in front of my face. "Drink up, sunshine."

I take in his ink and bare skin. The way the rays of sunshine bounce off the crevices of his muscles is so damn beautiful. "Maybe you should cover up," I tell him, taking the coffee from his hands.

Pike glances down, eyebrows furrowing. "I'll cover up when you do." His gaze flickers to my breasts, but it's so freaking hot, there's no way in hell I'm putting on any more layers.

I look around the beach, noticing the women eyeing my man, totally fantasizing about him. "Women are staring at you," I tell him before taking a sip of the iced coffee my body and mind need to function.

"Um—" he glances around "—the men are eye-fucking all three of you in your string bikinis, but you don't hear me complaining."

I roll my eyes, and Tamara giggles, followed by Lily's laughter. "We aren't wearing string bikinis," I tell him, moaning right afterward as I take another sip.

"Darlin', make that noise again, and the ladies are going to see more than my chest," he warns me, giving no fucks about the other women around us.

I raise my eyebrows before my eyes go right to his crotch. "Maybe we should go in the water. It's getting a little hot."

He waggles his eyebrows with a smirk.

"You two are gross," Tamara teases. "I'm not coming in there if you two fool around."

"There was more come on that couch last night than there is in that ocean," Pike tells her, not able to keep a straight face when she winces.

"Fuckin' gross," she mutters.

"Biker life," I tell her, hoping to warn her off Crow as I set my coffee in the sand and follow Pike toward the water.

"What's that about?" Pike asks, tipping his head back.

I link my hand with his, walking as fast as I can across the sand, which is as hot as lava from the sun overhead. "She's texting Crow."

Pike stops, and I almost fall forward as his hand locks around mine, holding me in place. "What did you say?" he growls.

I pull him forward, dancing in place because my feet are practically on fire. "I'll tell you once we're in the water unless you don't like my feet with skin."

"Skin's good," he mumbles like he's thrown.

Pike is never thrown. Never at a loss for words. But I can tell something is weighing on his mind.

"What's wrong?" I ask him, letting out a loud sigh when my toes finally hit the wet, cool sand near the water's edge.

"I don't like her with Crow," he admits. "A girl like her with a guy like him is nothing but trouble."

I wade into the water, letting my fingertips graze the tops of the waves as we wade deeper. "Tell me about him."

I don't ask about the *a girl like her* comment because I know he doesn't mean anything bad. He knows Tamara has a good heart, but he also knows she's much, much wilder than I ever could've been.

He doesn't say anything, just stares straight ahead as the waves crash nearby.

I tug on his arm, wanting his attention and his words. "Tell me." I smile, dipping my lower body into the water until just my breasts are bobbing on the surface.

He glances down, seeing my sweat-dotted breasts moving across the waves, and smiles. "Darlin', how am I supposed to say anything when you're tempting me like that?"

"Be a good boy and tell me what you know about Crow, and maybe you won't have to walk out of here sporting that hard-on I know is under the waves." I wink, being totally playful because there's a darkness in his eyes.

He lunges forward, wrapping his arms around my waist and smashing my breasts into his chest. I gasp, trying not to swallow the salty water as his lips find my neck, sucking the spot that always makes me pant. "I love when you think you're the boss," he whispers against my skin.

"I am the boss," I tell him, wrapping my legs around his middle, grinding my pussy against his hard cock. "Now tell me about Crow."

"Bossy as fuck," he murmurs against my skin, and I laugh, hooking my ankles and digging my heels into his ass.

Damn, I love this man.

23

PIKE

"THIS PLACE BRINGS BACK MEMORIES," Tamara says, winking at me across the table. "Am I right?"

I laugh even though it feels like a lifetime ago. Watching Gigi for what felt like hours, waiting for the girl to finally make her move. "Great memories," I mutter behind the mouth of the beer bottle in my hand.

Gigi snorts. "I remember nothing."

"You're a shit liar," Tamara tells her, shaking her head. "You weren't that drunk."

"Drunk enough to pass out," I add, earning me a glare from Gigi.

"Shut up," she tells me, but she's totally being playful. She's relaxed since our talk about Crow yesterday and then having words with her cousin about the man.

Maybe they worked shit out. Hopefully what I said to Gigi that she then passed on to Tamara put things into perspective.

"It's a shame Austin and Lily aren't here," Gigi says softly, turning the beer bottle in her hands.

"They're lightweights. I mean, who wants to stay in the room and binge-watch *Game of Thrones*?" Tamara blanches.

"They're nerds, Tam, and it's probably best that Austin isn't here. Kids really shouldn't hang out in bars."

Tamara bends her head back, slapping her hand on the table. "Jesus fuck, when did you turn into Suzy?"

I close my eyes and dig my fingertips into my eyes, knowing Tamara said the one thing that can set Gigi off quicker than a firecracker.

Gigi jerks her head back. "You're an asshole."

"Well." Tamara shrugs. "You just referred to Austin as a child, and the last time I checked, he's almost a grown man."

"Almost," I grumble, lifting my head and opening my eyes. "He's still in high school, and if I catch him at a bar…"

"You going to spank him?" Tamara raises an eyebrow, and I swear to God, the girl is just trying to get a rise out of me.

"Are you perpetually bored?" I glare at her.

She snorts, scrunching her nose. "You two are like two old biddies. I swear you're a perfect match."

Gigi slides her warm palm across my arm, making it impossible for me to keep the sour look on my face. "Ignore her. We know we're awesome." She smiles, and that face could light up an entire room.

"You know who's awesome?" Tamara asks, looking over my shoulder as a smirk plays on her lips.

Gigi turns, her fingers tightening around my arms.

"Don't say it," I mutter, knowing exactly who they're looking at.

Goddamn this girl.

Gigi's head snaps back to her cousin, dropping low to the table. "You invited him?" she hisses and somehow avoids yelling, even though I know she wants to.

Tamara nods. "Just for a few drinks. The compound isn't too far away, and he said he was missing me."

My jaw tightens as I curl my free hand into a fist, every muscle in my body so tight, I could snap.

"Fuck," Gigi hisses. "You're such a dumbass."

"Just be nice. We leave tomorrow, and I'll never see him again." Tamara pouts like that shit will work on me, but I'm not her parents, and it has no effect.

"You're not leaving with him," I tell her, pointing at her across the table with one finger, while the others are curled around the beer bottle.

"Yes, Dad," she groans and rolls her eyes. "Don't get your granny panties in a wad."

This has to be the painful agony of what being a parent feels like. The constant push and pull of doing the right thing and trying to give your child enough freedom to live, but not enough to hang themselves with. Tamara had to be a trying kid. I don't know how Anthony is still alive after twenty-one years of her constant need to be an asshole.

"Hey, sexy," Tamara greets him, rising to her feet as soon as Crow's within a few feet of our table.

He slides his bare arm around her waist, pulling her in like they're long-lost lovers. "I missed you, doll," he says softly, rubbing his beard against her neck, causing her to break out in a fit of girlish giggles.

"I'm going to vomit," Gigi mutters, placing her hand on my knee and squeezing hard.

They embrace for far too long, nuzzling into each other's necks, touching like they're more than just friends. "I'm so happy you came," Tamara adds as she grabs at his beard, holding his eyes. "So, so happy."

"I'd come anywhere for you, sweet lips." He winks.

"Crow." I interrupt their conversation when Gigi groans again at my side.

"Her father's going to murder us first," she says, shaking her head. "We're so dead."

"What are we drinking?" Crow asks, glancing down at the table with his arms still wrapped around Tamara. "Next round is on me."

"Isn't he sweet?" Tamara looks right at me, but I give her nothing, so she goes back to gawking at the bearded man with eyes as dark as coal. "He's the best ever. Come on, baby. I'll help you carry the beer for Grandpa and Grandma."

Crow furrows his eyebrows, but he just shrugs, letting her pull him into the crowd.

Gigi sighs, resting her head on my shoulder. "She's really trying to kill us."

I let out a small laugh and lean over, kissing the top of her head. "It'll be fine. A few drinks and his eyes will wander. He'll forget about her by tomorrow."

Gigi peers up at me, those blue eyes searching my face. "Did you forget about me so easily?"

"Fuck no, darlin'. I missed you the moment you left."

She gives me the biggest smile, making my insides warm. "Me too," she lies.

"You didn't call," I remind her.

She coughs, glancing down at her hands. "I was embarrassed."

"About?" I ask.

She shrugs. "I'd never had a one-night stand."

"It wasn't one night," I say, unable to wipe the smile off my face, remembering the endless days we spent wrapped around each other.

Gigi giggles, and it's still the sweetest sound I've ever heard. "I remember, old man. Will life ever be that easy again?"

I sigh, wrapping my arm around the back of her chair, playing with the ends of her hair with my fingertips. "I don't know, baby. But as long as you're at my side, I'll weather the bad any day to get to all the good."

"We got beer," Tamara announces as Crow sets down a metal bucket of beer and ice in the middle of the table.

"Drink up," Crow tells us as he turns a chair around, wrapping his upper body over the back as he sits, holding a glass of water in one hand.

"You're not drinking?" Tamara asks, mouth hanging open as she looks at the man at her side.

He shakes his head. "I'm driving tonight. Booze and bikes don't mix, doll."

That's the first thing to come out of his mouth that has me thinking maybe he isn't the biggest tool in the shed.

"You can crash in my room," she offers, pushing the bucket in his direction.

He glances my way and shakes his head. "I think it's best if I don't."

And again, he's being smart. There was no way in hell I was going to let him stay in her room. I don't care how old she is; it would've been a hard no. Well, I would've put Austin in there too, which would've been an instant mood-killer.

"I understand," she says, eyeing me across the table. "Maybe next time."

"Sure, doll. Next time," he mutters.

"So, Crow," Gigi mutters. "Did you grow up in New York?"

He shakes his head, smiling as Tamara touches his arm and runs the tips of her fingernails back and forth. "I was a military brat. We moved around a lot."

"Have any brothers or sisters?" she asks immediately after he answers.

"One brother, no sisters."

"Do you have a job?" she asks as she reaches into the bucket, fishing out a fresh beer.

Crow dips his hand into his back pocket and tosses his wallet near Gigi. "Tamara told me about your uncles. Feel free to have them check into me."

Gigi scrunches her nose. He called her out, knowing she was interrogating him.

Tamara snorts. "She won't do that, baby."

Gigi takes the wallet, flipping it open and scanning the contents. "Logan Taylor," she says, pulling out his driver's license and tapping her index finger against the top.

"That's my name," he says to her, still smiling as he runs his fingers over his beard.

"Logan's a sexy name too, baby," Tamara adds. "But Crow's totally badass."

Crow turns his face toward Tamara, smile never wavering. "You call me whatever you want, sweet lips."

I take his wallet and driver's license from Gigi's hands, putting everything back the way it was when she opened the damn thing. "Leave the man alone."

She gapes at me in total disbelief.

I toss the wallet back in his direction. "They're just friends."

Gigi blinks before shaking her head. "What are you doing?" she whispers in my ear.

I place my fingers on the side of her neck, turning her head so I have her ear. "You want to drive her into his arms?"

"No," she whispers against my skin.

"Then stop being a cockblock. What happened when your parents hated someone?" I ask her.

"Point taken," she groans and backs away, gaze moving toward her cousin. "Want to go dance with me, Tam?"

"No," Tamara replies, too busy with her hands all over Crow.

Gigi stands, rounding the table before pulling on Tamara's arm. "Yeah, you do. You love to dance.

Don't you want to show Crow all your moves?" Gigi shakes her hips.

I want to pull her back into the chair, tell her she's not shaking that fine thing for all these bastards, but I don't.

"Do you care?" Tamara peers down at Crow, looking for permission.

"Shake away," he says, tipping his chin toward the small dance floor.

"Want to come?" She wiggles her fingers at him, but he shakes his head. "Your loss, baby."

I glare at Crow, watching him as he gawks at Tamara's ass. "Why are you here?" I ask him as soon as the girls hit the dance floor.

He shrugs, lifting his water to his lips, giving zero fucks that I don't want him here. "Just trying to hold on to that goodness."

I lean forward, setting my beer to the side and clearing a space in front of me. "While I understand wanting to hold on to that goodness, there's definitely a line you're crossing."

"A line?" he asks, slinging his arm over the chair and placing his glass of water down in front of him. "She asked me to come and have a drink. It was either come here or hang with the guys, watching them as they got shit-faced. What would you have done?"

"Crow, baby. Watch!" Tamara yells, turning

around as soon as he glances in her direction and shaking her ass in a way that doesn't say friends at all.

"Fuck," he hisses, but not from being pissed off.

"Crow, listen." I take a deep breath, trying not to be a hypocrite because, fuck, I've been there. I've been drawn in by all the sweetness, almost getting Gigi killed in the process. "Your life doesn't mesh with hers." I turn my head toward Gigi and Tamara, laughing and bouncing to the old eighties metal song coming out of the oversized speakers. "She's everything you think. Sweet and all that shit, but she isn't for you. She'll never be for you."

He narrows his eyes, studying my face as he tosses his thumb over his shoulder. "And your girl?"

"I don't deserve her. I don't think I ever will. But we've been to hell and back together."

"Tamara said you two work together."

Tamara's a little too chatty, especially with a complete stranger. "We do now."

"And you used to live at the compound."

I nod, keeping all emotion from my face.

"She told me all about you, Pike. All about her family too."

My knee starts to shake as I force myself to stay seated. "They wouldn't like you either."

He gives me a shit-eating grin. "Never met a family who didn't love me."

"What are you doing with a kid like her?"

"Kid?" He laughs. "She's not a kid. Look at her. Isn't she the same age as your girl?"

I scan the dance floor, catching sight of Tamara and Gigi shaking their hips and tits for everyone to see. There's nothing childish about them besides their ability to bicker and sometimes be annoying as fuck.

"They're a year apart," I tell him, swallowing because I know I'm being an asshole.

"I get where you're coming from. I know you don't want my dirt to blow back on her, have her running for her life."

I know that's a dig at me. I'm sure Crow knows all about the men who were lost in the Disciples from the attack by DiSantis's men.

"I'm not like most of the guys in the club. I stick to myself. I do what's needed when I'm asked and am loyal as fuck, but I'm not into the club whores, drugs, and drinking every day scene. I work my ass off working on cars, saving my money for when I get an old lady." He turns his head toward Tamara, the smile back on his face. "I want some goodness in my life someday too. But I know that girl—" he pauses for a second and looks back at me "—is a wild one and isn't looking to settle down. I'm not here to break her heart. I'm not here to turn her bad. I saved her from some bad shit with Lefty, and you know it." He points at me, and I resist the urge to bat his hand away. "She asked me to come, so I'm here. Tomorrow, she'll move on, putting her crazy love on someone else. But tonight, I'm soaking up her sweetness, storing it away for the times I need to remember I'm more than just a soldier in someone else's army."

"Get your fuckin' hands off me!" Gigi screeches from the dance floor, her voice carrying over the music.

The guy has a lopsided smile, not seeming to care that she's batting his hands away.

I'm out of my seat before she can say another word, Crow's loud bootsteps right behind me.

I grab the guy by the collar, hauling him backward until he stumbles, almost falling over. "The lady said hands off."

"Who the fuck are you?" he croaks, slurring his words and spitting at the same time.

"Her man," I tell him, twisting the material around his neck so tightly, I know he's losing oxygen.

"Incoming!" Crow yells out as Tamara and Gigi are pushed backward, and a small group of men steps forward.

"The fuck you touchin' him, man?"

Here we go. There's never a dull moment. Never a simple evening out. Never any peace.

The guy in my clutches swings on me, and I sweep my leg out, taking his feet out from under him.

"Oh fuck," Gigi hisses, eyes wide as the other men move toward us, fists in the air.

"I got you," Crow says at my side.

Mass chaos breaks out. Fists, legs, chairs, and just about everything movable goes flying in the bar. It's like something out of *Roadhouse*.

As my fist connects with a guy's face, I search the crowd while Tamara and Gigi head toward the door, hands over their heads to protect themselves.

"You messed with the wrong motherfuckers," Crow tells one of the guys before landing a wicked uppercut, causing the man's head to snap back in a completely unnatural way.

In this moment, I've never been happier to have the bastard by my side.

"Son of a bitch."

My eyes snap open, and I wince as the sunlight streams through the open curtains. "What's wrong?"

I turn, seeing Gigi holding a small sheet of paper, her eyes wide and mouth hanging open.

"The bitch did it. I'm going to kill her." Gigi starts pacing, shaking her head.

"Did what? Who?" I ask, rubbing the sleep from my eyes before lifting up on my elbows.

"Tamara," she whispers as she stops moving, gaping at the paper in disbelief.

"What did she do?" I ask again.

Gigi shoves the piece of paper in my face. "Read it."

Cover for me!
I'm chasing my
epic adventure.
—Tam xoxo

I hope you loved Burn, the continuation of Pike and Gigi's story. ***The ride isn't over***... Tamara Gallo's a wild one and her story is coming next in Wildfire.

Visit *menofinked.com/wildfire* for more information.

Dear Reader,

I'd love to say *Burn* was easy to write. But that would be a straight up lie. I know how hard you fell in love with Gigi & Pike in Flame and the pressure to follow that awesomeness was intense. But in the end, I wrote my little heart out, giving you happiness, insanity, and some sexy fun along the way.

I love living in the Men of Inked world. The Gallos are such an amazing family filled with love, laughter, and ball-busting fun. There's always some parts of my crazy Italian family sprinkled into every story too.

The Men of Inked Heatwave isn't over though. There are THIRTEEN kids from the original Men of Inked series. Phew! That's a lot.

I'm a lot like Gigi, a complete Daddy's girl and sassy. But one thing I know…my mom is not Suzy. Rose is even sassier and she'll throw down with words any day of the week. She think she's the head honcho in the family, but then again… her two sisters probably think they are too.

If you loved Gigi & Pike, please consider leaving a review or letting your reader friends about the Gallos. That would be super sweet and totally cool of you.

If you love my writing and want to know when the next Gallo book releases:

- Sign up for my Newsletter

- Follow me on Bookbub
- Text GALLOS to 24587
- Join my Private Facebook Reader Group

If you're new to me and are looking for your next favorite read, check out Throttle Me — Joe Gallo's story. Gigi's father is where everything started and he's a super alpha.

If you've already read Throttle Me, check out my other free reads.

Mad Love,

Chelle *xoxo*

Want more Men of Inked?

Thank you for reading Burn! I hope you love the Gallo Family as much as I do. Want to start at the beginning?

Download Throttle Me Now

MORE BOOKS BY CHELLE BLISS

View Chelle's entire collection of books at
menofinked.com/books

Original Men of Inked Series

Join the Gallo siblings as their lives are turned upside down by irresistible chemistry and unexpected love. A sizzling USA Today bestselling series!

Throttle Me - Book 1 (Free Download)

Ambitious Suzy has her life planned out, but everything changes when she meets tattooed bad boy **Joseph Gallo**. Could their one-night stand ever turn into the real thing?

Hook Me - Book 2

Michael Gallo has been working toward his dream of winning a MMA championship, but when he meets a sexy doctor who loathes violence, his plans may get derailed.

Resist Me - Book 3

After growing up with four older brothers, **Izzy Gallo** refuses to be ordered around by anyone. So when hot, bossy James Caldo saves her from trouble, will she be able to give up control?

Uncover Me - Book 4

Roxanne has been part of the dangerous Sun Devils motorcycle club all of her life, while **Thomas Gallo** has been deep undercover for so long, he's forgotten who he truly is. Can they find redemption and save each other?

Without Me - Book 5

Anthony Gallo never thought he'd fall in love, but when he meets the only woman who doesn't fall to her knees in front of him, he's instantly smitten.

Honor Me - Book 6

Joe and Suzy Gallo have everything they ever wanted and are living the American dream. Just when life has evened out, a familiar enemy comes back to haunt them.

Worship Me - Book 7

James Caldo needs to control everything in his life, even his wife. But **Izzy Gallo**'s stubborn and is constantly testing her husband's limits as much as he pushes hers.

Men of Inked: Heatwave Series

The Gallo's Next Generation

Flame - Book 1

Gigi Gallo's childhood was filled with the roar of a

motorcycle and the hum of a tattoo gun. Fresh out of college, she never expected to run into someone tall, dark, and totally sexy from her not-so-innocent past.

Burn - Book 2

Gigi Gallo thought she'd never fall in love, but then he rode into her world covered in ink and wrapped in chaos. Pike Moore never expected his past to follow him into his future, but nothing stays hidden for long.

Wildfire - Book 3

Tamara Gallo knew she was missing something in life. Looking for adventure, she takes off, searching for a hot biker who can deliver more than a good time. But once inside the Disciples, she may get more than she bargained for.

Men of Inked: Southside Series

The Chicago side of the Gallo Family

Maneuver - Book 1

Poor single mother Delilah is suspicious when sexy **Lucio Gallo** offers her and her baby a place to live. But soon the muscular bar owner is working his way into her heart — and into her bed…

Flow - Book 2

The moment **Daphne Gallo** looked into his eyes, she knew she was in trouble. Their fathers were enemies--Chicago crime bosses from rival families. But that didn't stop Leo Conti from pursuing her.

Hook - Book 3

Nothing prepared **Angelo Gallo** for losing his wife. He promised her that he'd love again. Find someone to mend his broken heart. And that seemed impossible, until the day that he walked into Tilly Carter's cupcake shop.

Hustle - Book 4

Vinnie Gallo's the hottest rookie in professional football. He's a smooth-talker, good with his hands, and knows how to score. Nothing will stop Vinnie from getting the girl—not a crazy stalker or the fear he's falling in love.

Love - Book 5

Finding love once is hard, but twice is almost impossible. **Angelo Gallo** had almost given up, but then Tilly Carter walked into his life and the sweet talkin' Southern girl stole his heart forever.

ALFA Investigations Series

A sexy, suspenseful Men of Inked Spin-off series…

Sinful Intent - Book 1

Out of the army and back to civilian life, **Morgan DeLuca** takes a job with a private investigation firm. When he meets his first client, one night of passion blurs the line between business and pleasure...

Unlawful Desire - Book 2

Frisco Jones was never lucky in love and had finally given up, diving into his new job at ALFA Investigations. But when a dirty-mouthed temptress crossed his path, he questioned everything.

Wicked Impulse - Book 3

Bear North, ALFA's resident bad boy, had always lived by the friend's code of honor—Never sleep with a buddy's sister, and family was totally off-limits. But that was before **Fran DeLuca**, his best friend's mom, seduced him.

Guilty Sin - Book 5

When a mission puts a woman under **Ret North**'s protection, he and his longtime girlfriend Alese welcome her into their home. What starts out as a friendship rooted in trust ignites into a romance far bigger than any of them expect.

Single Novels

Enshrine

When Callie's life crumbles around her, can she trust her attraction to ruthless Bruno?

Mend

Before senior year, I was forced to move away, leaving behind the only man I ever loved. He promised he'd love me forever. He vowed nothing would tear us apart. He swore he'd wait for me, but Jack lied.

Rebound

After having his heart broken, **Flash** heads to New Orleans to lose himself, but ends up finding so much more!

Acquisition - Takeover 1

Rival CEO Antonio Forte is arrogant, controlling, and sexy as hell. He'll stop at nothing to get control of Lauren's company.The only problem? He's also the one-night stand she can't forget. And Antonio not only wants her company, he wants her as part of the acquisition.

Merger - Takeover 2

Antonio Forte has always put business before pleasure, but ever since he met the gorgeous CEO of Interstellar Corp, he finds himself wanting both. And he's hoping she won't be able to refuse his latest offer.

Top Bottom Switch

Ret North knows exactly who he is—a Dominant male with an insatiable sexual appetite. He's always been a top, searching for his bottom…until a notorious switch catches his eye.

Love at Last Series

Untangle Me - Book 1

Kayden is a bad boy that never played by the rules. **Sophia** has always been the quintessential good girl, living a life filled with disappointment. Everything changes when their lives become intertwined through a chance encounter online.

Kayden the Past - Book 2

Kayden Michaels has a past filled with sex, addiction, and heartache. Needing to get his addictions in check and gain control of his life for the sake of his family, Kayden is forced to confront his past and make amends for the path he's walked.

Do you LOVE audiobooks?

To check out my entire audio library, please visit menofinked.com/audio for more information.

Get a Text Audio Alert
Text **AUDIO** to **24587**
USA Only

Want the latest audiobook news and special giveaways! Join here: menofinked.com/audionews

ABOUT THE AUTHOR

Chelle hails from the Ohio, but currently lives near the beach in Florida even though she hates sand.

She's a full-time writer, time-waster extraordinaire, social media addict, coffee fiend, and ex-history teacher.

She loves spending time with her two cats, sometimes pain in the ass alpha boyfriend, and chatting with readers.

To learn more about Chelle's books, please visit menofinked.com.

Text Notifications (US only)

➔ Text **BLISS** to **24587**

Want to drop me a line?

authorchellebliss@gmail.com

menofinked.com

Where to Follow Me:

facebook.com/authorchellebliss1
bookbub.com/authors/chelle-bliss
instagram.com/authorchellebliss
twitter.com/ChelleBliss1
goodreads.com/chellebliss
amazon.com/author/chellebliss
pinterest.com/chellebliss10

ACKNOWLEDGMENTS

I don't even know where to start. Writing the acknowledgements are fucking hard. Like my head is ready to explode at the amount of mental energy. So, I'm going to keep this simple.

Thank you to every person who helped me with Burn.

- Readers: you're the best damn people in the world.
- Friends, betas, ARC readers: you're the bees knees.
- Brian: thanks for putting up with my crankiness.

I know there's more, but my brain is dead and I need a nap.

...Keep on going Gallo Girl. There's more to come!

Lightning Source UK Ltd.
Milton Keynes UK
UKHW041558160521
383755UK00014B/34

9 781950 023837